Conflict

Kathy wondered if she should ask Deena's advice. Maybe she would know how to handle Roy and Ellecia, and Ken's friends, too. Deena was really on Ken's wavelength. Kathy had noticed that from the few times she'd overheard them talking about school, or skiing, or other things that interested them both.

Bag that idea, Kathy thought as she punched up her pillow again. Deena would go into her know-it-all "Dear Abby" act, and she would never let Kathy forget that she'd come to her for advice. No, she wouldn't ask Deena for advice about this. She'd simply have to work it out on her own.

Cranberry Cousins
SECRET CRUSH

BY CHRISTIE WELLS

A Troll Book

Library of Congress Cataloging-in-Publication Data

Wells, Christie.
    Secret crush / by Christie Wells.
      p.   cm.—(The Cranberry cousins; #2)
    Summary: The normally tense relationship between two cousins whose
mothers run Cranberry Inn worsens when one starts dating a boy the
other has a secret crush on.
    ISBN 0-8167-1498-3 (lib. bdg.)   ISBN 0-8167-1499-1 (pbk.)
    [1. Cousins—Fiction.]   I. Title.   II. Series: Wells, Christie.
Cranberry cousins; #2.
PZ7.W4635Se   1989
[Fic]—dc19   88-16941

A TROLL BOOK, published by Troll Associates
Mahwah, NJ 07430

Printed in the United States of America.
10   9   8   7   6   5   4   3   2   1

Chapter 1

"Rise and shine." Deena stood beside Kathy's bed and gave her cousin a shake. "Come on, sleepy-head. Looks like a beautiful day out there!"

Kathy responded with a sleepy moan, then burrowed deeper under her covers. "Beautiful day? Are you crazy? It's still dark outside. It's the middle of the night..." Closing her eyes again, she rolled over to face the wall.

"It's already six-thirty, Kathy. Didn't you hear the alarm? Hey!" Deena gave her another, more forceful prod. "Time to hit the slopes!" she said brightly.

Hit the slopes! The only thing Kathy had the urge to hit just then was her disgustingly cheerful cousin. How could anyone sound so chipper at this unholy hour? It just wasn't normal.

"Five more minutes please," she begged in a muffled voice. "I'll be up like a shot, promise."

"Kathy, you said that five minutes ago." Deena knew that getting Kathy moving this morning would be a challenge. But this was ridiculous. If Kathy didn't get up soon, Deena thought she was going to have to resort to some drastic measures. Like yanking off her covers, or blasting her with some Beethoven. Classical music made Kathy's skin crawl—she definitely couldn't sleep through that.

Hands on her hips, Deena stared down at the inert lump under the covers. She had more or less forced Kathy to sign up for the ski trip. She hoped to get her cousin involved in some athletic activity that was more enriching than fighting for tickets to a rock concert. She thought it would be good for Kathy to try something different for a change. Now she wasn't so sure.

Ever since their mothers had decided to reopen the old Cranberry Inn, Kathy and Deena had struggled to get along. They disagreed over just about everything. This morning was no exception.

Slowly lifting her head up off the pillow, Kathy gave Deena a sleepy glare. Even half-awake she noticed that Deena was already completely dressed for their day at Briarwood Mountain. In her powder-blue bib overalls, with white turtleneck and matching headband, she looked like she had stepped right off the pages of *Ski* magazine. The colors complimented Deena's blond hair and blue eyes perfectly. Kathy had to admit her cousin was cute—if you liked that preppie, Ivory Soap-girl look. Which Kathy certainly did *not*.

Kathy flopped back against her pillows. "I can't believe you're dressed already. What did you do, sleep in those clothes?"

"Don't be ridiculous," Deena huffed. She tucked an errant strand of her honey-blond hair back under her headband. "Just because some people are efficient and self-disciplined enough to get up at a decent hour so that they can be punctual—"

Kathy moaned again and yanked the pillow over her head. "Stop! Please! I give up! Anything but a predawn lecture from Cranford's very own Miss Manners. I'm getting up. See?" Kathy finally sat up in bed, feeling around the cold floor with her feet for her slippers.

"You know, Deena, you never told me we had to join Dawn Patrol in order to go on this trip. Pretty sneaky of you," Kathy observed, tugging on the huge T-shirt she had slept in. It had Bruce Springsteen's picture on one side and said BORN IN THE USA on the other. "And don't tell me you just forgot, because I won't believe you."

Deena cocked her head to one side, watching Kathy fumble her way into her bathrobe. "Well, I'll admit that I purposely left that small detail out the other day, knowing how you like to sleep late on Saturdays and waste the entire day. But honestly, Kath, isn't it wonderful to get up with the sun? To say good morning to the birds? Just like Thoreau at Walden Pond—remember? We read it in

Mrs. Godfrey's class?" Deena walked over to the window near Kathy's bed and flung open the curtains. "Hello, sun! Hello, birds!"

Kathy just stared at her, then yanked the belt on her bathrobe tighter. "It's pitch black out there, and the only bird I've spotted so far is a cuckoo in ski pants. Why did I ever agree to go on this dumb trip?"

Shaking her head, she stalked around the room, trying to collect the clothes she was going to wear. She honestly could not remember right now why she had ever agreed to go skiing with Deena in the first place. Deena had come home from school a few days ago in raptures about the recent snowfall and the trip the ski club at school was running. She started bragging about what a great skier she was and how she couldn't wait to get started and weren't they just incredibly lucky to have such an early snowfall this year! Then she asked Kathy if she wanted to come along and try it out. She told her that it would be a good way to meet some really *nice* people for a change. Which was pretty mean, Kathy thought, since her friend Roy was sitting right there and heard everything. Roy was too nice to make a big deal out of it, even though Kathy could tell it had hurt his feelings.

As usual, Kathy knew Deena was trying to be nice, but her cousin's whole attitude just pushed all the wrong buttons. Kathy had never put on a pair of skis in her life. But just to shut Deena up, Kathy told her that she already knew how to ski and certainly didn't need any private lessons from her. Then, one thing led to another, and

4

pretty soon Kathy was agreeing to go on the dumb ski trip.

Tossing her clothes on her unmade bed, Kathy dragged herself toward the bathroom. Deena followed, pleased that Kathy was finally showing some signs of life. "Don't take too long getting dressed now. We need to have a good breakfast, something nourishing. How does Wheatena sound?"

"Repulsive!" Kathy spun around in the bathroom doorway. "I'll have my usual breakfast, thanks."

"A glass of grapefruit juice and a Twinkie? Not exactly a wholesome meal," Deena said patiently. "Skiing is strenuous exercise. You need to eat something hot and substantial."

Kathy considered her cousin's advice. "O.K.—make me a cup of Swiss Miss and put the Twinkie in the microwave. I'll be down in a minute." She smiled sweetly and shut the door.

The room that Kathy and Deena shared was on the third floor. Deena quietly crept down to the second floor, then went down the back staircase that led directly to the kitchen, being careful not to wake up anyone else in the house.

In September Deena had moved from Boston with her mother to live in the Cranberry Inn with her cousins Kathy and Johnny and her aunt Nancy, who was Deena's mother's sister. The Delaney sisters had inherited the rambling old Victorian mansion from their grandparents. But the inn had been closed for many years, until

Deena's mother had gotten the idea of fixing up the place and reopening it. She had persuaded Kathy's mother to give it a try.

Aunt Nancy and Deena's cousins were then living in San Francisco. They arrived at the inn in a dusty red van a few days after Deena and her mother had come down from Boston. It was impossible at first for Deena to get along with her cousin—and new roommate—Kathy. The only thing they agreed on was that they disagreed on everything. It hadn't helped matters much when their English teacher, Mrs. Godfrey, dubbed them the Cranberry Cousins during one of their first days at school. They were *never* going to live *that* down! At first they fought so much they disrupted the whole household. Their mothers nearly decided to give up the entire plan just because Deena and Kathy couldn't get along. After that, they called a truce and managed somehow to be a bit more tolerant of each other, although it was still rather difficult to do at times.

Deena got out all the ingredients she needed for the hot cereal and put a pot of water up to boil on the big black cast iron stove. She hoped the ski trip today with Kathy would go well and wouldn't provoke another world war between them. No matter what she did to try and improve things between them, it always seemed to blow up in her face. She hoped today would be different.

Upstairs, Kathy was almost finished dressing. Unlike Deena, Kathy was usually able to shower and dress quickly. It wasn't that she didn't care about her appearance. But unlike her cousin, she never looked as if she had *tried* to look great. *Crisp*, *preppie*, and *conservative*, were the words that would describe Deena's wardrobe. She liked to thumb through fashion magazines, and Princess Diana was probably at the top of Deena's best-dressed list. In contrast, *off-beat*, *quirky*, and *hip* were apt descriptions of Kathy's clothes. She never read fashion magazines and got most of her outfit ideas from the music videos of her favorite rock stars. But she had the knack for throwing together an outfit that looked just right.

Needless to say, each of the girls thought the *other* could do a lot to improve her appearance. Sometimes they tried to give each other subtle hints. Other times, like this morning, the hints were not so subtle.

"You're wearing *that* to go skiing?" Deena had been spooning some hot cereal into a bowl on the counter. At the sight of Kathy, the spoon slipped out of her hand and landed on the counter with a loud *splat*. There was warm, nutritious Wheatena everywhere.

Kathy looked down at herself. She had on a pair of tight black jeans and a huge white sweater that had Oakfield Angels and a pair of wings embroidered in red letters across the front. It was the name of the football team at Kathy's old school in California. She also wore a long red scarf wrapped around her neck. The color looked good with her straight, glossy brown hair and big dark eyes. To complete the outfit she had sunglasses tucked into a pocket on her sweater and a black cowboy cap in hand, just in case her head got cold. "What's wrong with what I have on? I think I look fine."

"Well, for one thing," Deena said, wiping Wheatena off her overalls, "those jeans are going to get soaked when you fall." She didn't bother to add that they would also probably split right up the middle.

"I don't fall much," Kathy said, crossing her arms over her chest.

Just like Deena to assume she'd be tripping all over herself, turning into a human snowball. Kathy had never skied before, but she was a pretty good dancer and great on a skateboard, so she didn't think she'd have all that much trouble. The truth was, she had sprayed the jeans with water repellant last night—the kind her mother used on old raincoats—and also had on a pair of long underwear, which was why the jeans looked so tight. But she didn't have to tell Deena that. It was fun to drive her cousin a little crazy sometimes—well, *most* of the time, really.

Deena just shrugged. "Well, it's too late to change anyway," she said, glancing up at the clock. "We'd better hurry up and eat. Jessie's mother should be here any minute."

The two girls hurriedly ate their breakfast—Kathy finally gave in and shared the hot cereal. When they heard Jessie's mother's station wagon pull into the inn's driveway, they grabbed their hats and gloves and dashed out the kitchen door.

By the time they arrived at the high school, a large group had already assembled in the parking lot. Kathy couldn't believe so many people had the will power to get up this early on a Saturday just to strap a lot of heavy, awkward equipment to their feet and roll around in the freezing cold snow.

"Come on, Deena. Let's get our seats," Kathy said, walking toward the bus. "You can have the window," she generously offered. "I think I'm going to take a nap."

"Wait!" Deena grabbed Kathy's arm. "There's Ken Buckly. He's the president of the ski club," she whispered, sounding to Kathy as if she had just spotted Tom Cruise. "He's really cute, don't you think?" Kathy glanced over at him. He was tall, blond, and quite athletic-looking—especially in his red one-piece ski outfit. The red jumpsuit had white stripes down the arms and legs and made him look like a race car driver. Patches from various ski resorts and the high school ski club were sewn across the front of his coveralls.

Some of the other ski club members were loading equipment into the bottom of the bus. Ken was holding a clipboard and checking off names. He looked very official and much too busy to notice Kathy and Deena's secret glances.

"Sure—he's O.K., I guess," Kathy replied with a shrug. "If you like the boy-scout type."

"He's very smart, too, and plays first French horn in the orchestra," Deena added, with more than a hint of adoration in her voice. "I mean, aside from being good-looking, junior class treasurer, and on the varsity track team."

"Yes, but does he know all the lyrics to 'Sub-Atomic

Attraction' by Nuclear Waste? I mean, there are certain *important* things you should look for when you fall for a guy, Deena," Kathy advised with a smile.

"I didn't say I had a crush on him," Deena denied. "I only said I thought he was cute." Deena really did have a crush on him—a mega-crush to be exact. But although she was sometimes tempted to confide such secrets in Kathy, she rarely did. She and Kathy could get along well enough on days like today. But she just didn't feel close enough to trust Kathy with a secret like that. "Guess we should let him know we're here," she said, determined to change the subject.

"I guess so," Kathy shrugged. "Let's go tell him." She started moving toward Ken, but Deena grabbed her arm again. "Uh—why don't I tell him, and you get our seat?"

"O.K." Kathy turned and began to walk away again, this time toward the bus. "No, wait," Deena said. "You can go tell him, and I'll get the seats." Deena glanced quickly over at Ken, who was nearby talking to another group of girls. She straightened her headband and yellow wool scarf. "Or maybe we should go tell him together."

Kathy was used to Deena spinning her wheels about the proper way to do things, but this was getting crazy. She groaned and jammed on her cowboy hat, the rim touching the top of her sunglasses. "I've got it—let's send him a Candygram."

Deena glared at her. She thought Kathy looked silly in that hat, but didn't say anything. She already knew how little her cousin valued her fashion advice.

"Howdy, ma'am. You must be a stranger in town," a

voice greeted Kathy in a Western drawl. "I don't think I checked your name off my list."

"Kathy, sir—Kathy Manelli," she answered, imitating his Western accent.

It was Ken, standing right next to them. Deena felt her mouth get dry. She checked her headband again to make sure it was straight. How had he snuck up on them without her noticing?

Ken scanned the list on his clipboard. "O.K., Kathy. You'll be renting equipment?" Kathy nodded. "And how about your horse?" he joked.

"My horse refused to get out of bed this early. So I came with her." Kathy flipped the end of her scarf over her shoulder and gestured toward Deena.

Laughing, Ken glanced over at Deena. He smiled at her, and Deena felt herself blush. She knew that Kathy and Ken weren't really laughing at her, but she somehow felt dumb after their clever conversation.

"Deena. Deena Scott," she said hurriedly before Ken had a chance to ask her name. "I have my own equipment—I'm a pretty advanced skier."

"Great." Ken nodded and searched his list for her name. Deena secretly studied him. His eyes were so blue. She liked the serious way he looked when he was thinking. Why did she just blurt out her name like that? As if she were reporting for duty in the army or something? She bit down on her lower lip. She was sure he thought she was a twerp—a total social clod!

"We'll be handing out the lift tickets right after we arrive. You can give this to the rental desk for your skis,

Kathy," Ken said, handing her a pink slip of paper. "Looks like a great day for skiing. See you on the slopes," he said, smiling at both of them—but more at Kathy, Deena thought.

"See you later, Ken," Deena said.

Kathy yawned. "Let's get on the bus, Deena. I'm losing crucial nap time."

How could Kathy even think of sleeping now, after talking to Ken Buckly for an entire five minutes? Deena was sure she wouldn't sleep for a week. But that was Kathy. She just couldn't appreciate someone like Ken. Ken was the complete opposite of Kathy's boyfriend, Roy Harris. All Roy cared about was cruising around town on his motorcycle and listening to rock 'n' roll. He was forever banging out the beat to a rock song on the handiest piece of furniture. It was so juvenile and annoying, but Kathy never seemed to mind. In fact, she looked as if she actually enjoyed it.

Once they had boarded the bus and found a place, Kathy flopped down in a seat on the aisle next to Deena and took out her Walkman.

"I was having the greatest dream when you woke me up this morning," she told Deena as she adjusted the headphones and put her hat back on over them. "It was the grand opening of the inn, and all these super-famous rock groups and their roadies checked in . . . " Kathy rattled off the names of a few new wave groups that made absolutely no sense to Deena, " . . . and they set up their equipment in the big front parlor and had this big jam session, right in the Cranberry Inn. Was that a great dream, or what?"

"Sounds like a nightmare to me," Deena said.

"It was mint," Kathy insisted, settling back in her seat. "The concert was called 'Cranberry Aid,' and everyone from town came. It was ten times better than that dumb open house our mothers are planning."

"The open house party will be just right. Welcoming, but elegant," Deena said. It would be too, if the inn was ready to receive guests by then. The old hotel was scheduled to open in about two weeks, on Thanksgiving Day, and everyone was working hard to get the place in shape. But there was so much fixing up left to do, some of the rooms almost did look as if there had been a rock concert on the premises.

Deena and Kathy had been doing their share of the repair work. But Deena had come to dread the inevitable squabbles every time they had so much as to clean up the kitchen together. That was really why she had asked Kathy along on this trip. They were always forced together whenever there was some irksome job to do. But since they both hung around with different groups of friends at school, they rarely spent any fun time together. Deena hoped that if they did a few more fun activities with each other, maybe they wouldn't fight so much.

Deena rubbed the frost off the window and looked out. As the bus pulled out she felt a surge of excitement. She secretly congratulated herself on getting Kathy to come along. So far the day had gotten off to a shaky start, but at least they weren't arguing. Of course, right now Kathy was almost asleep, Deena noticed as she glanced over at her.

With her hat tipped down over her nose, Kathy's sleepy thoughts drifted. Why did she even bother telling Deena about her dreams? Deena never thought they were interesting. Actually, if she did fall asleep on the bus ride, Kathy was almost sure she wouldn't have another rock concert dream, but one about skiing. She would be featured in the starring role, coming home with a broken leg. Now *that* would be a nightmare.

How was she going to get around telling Deena she couldn't ski? Maybe she could hide out in the lodge all day, watching the fire and sipping hot chocolate. No, Deena wouldn't let her get away with that one. But it was a pleasant thought. Pleasant enough for her to fall asleep as the bus headed for Briarwood Mountain.

Chapter 2

It was a scene of mass confusion when the bus arrived at the resort and everyone got off. Skis and poles flew in all directions. While Deena waited for her equipment to be unloaded from the bus, Kathy went over to the rental shop where she was fitted with everything she needed. Stumbling under the awkward load, she found her way out of the shop and met up with Deena at the lockers inside the ski lodge.

"Need some help putting your boots on?" Deena offered. She was already clipped up in her bright blue boots and was smearing some special lip gloss on her mouth.

"Are you kidding? I know how to put them on," Kathy assured Deena. The guy at the rental desk was very helpful. He explained everything, she added silently.

"Here's your lift ticket." Deena handed Kathy a blue ticket that had a metal fastener on one end. Deena clipped hers to the zipper of her down vest.

"Thanks." Kathy took a break from wrestling with the impossibly stubborn clips on her ski boot and fastened the ticket to her sweater.

"Gee—the lift line is long already," Deena said, glancing outside a big window which faced the slopes. "It's such a great day for skiing. Looks like the early snow really brought out the crowds."

"Why don't you go ahead, Deena? I'll catch up to you later."

Deena glanced wistfully at the skiers skimming down the hillside. "Well—if you're sure you don't need any help . . ."

"I'm fine. I just like to take my time putting the boots on. It kind of gets me in the mood," Kathy fibbed. If she could get rid of Deena for a while, Kathy thought she would sneak off and take a lesson. She'd read a sign in the ski shop and knew that a group beginner class was meeting in about fifteen minutes.

Deena picked up her skis and gloves. "O.K. I'll start and we'll meet up in a little while. I'll look for you at the bottom of the hill."

Try under that cluster of bushes, Kathy thought. She could so easily picture herself tangled up there. Everyone was shooting down that hill so fast. She just had to take a lesson. She'd never survive otherwise.

"I'll find you," Kathy assured her.

Deena smiled and slipped her amber ski goggles down over her eyes. "See you later." Just outside the lodge, Kathy watched as her cousin stepped into her skis and neatly glided off in the direction of the lift line.

Deena had a niggling feeling of guilt at leaving Kathy alone. After all, the whole idea of this trip was to hang out and have fun together. But Kathy was such a slow-poke sometimes; especially when she didn't want to do something. Deena skied up to the lift and took her place in line. Kathy would catch up in a little while, she assured herself. She glanced around, seeing a few people from the trip, but no sign of Ken. Maybe she would catch up to him later, too, she thought with a secret smile.

After watching Deena glide away so effortlessly, Kathy tackled her boots again. She couldn't even handle the stupid equipment. She was going to make a complete fool of herself, and Deena would know for sure that she'd been lying about being a good skier. How did she get herself into these situations? Deena seemed to have a knack for bringing out the worst in her.

Kathy attacked the stubborn buckles with a new surge of energy, then put on the other boot. She was fuming over the last two clips when she felt someone tap the brim of her cowboy hat.

She looked up to see Ken. He was wearing his ski boots, but carrying his skis and poles over his shoulder. "Having trouble with that?"

"A little," Kathy admitted.

"These rental boots are always tricky." Ken put his

skis down, then knelt down to help her. "Bend your knees and lean forward against the front of the boot."

Kathy did as she was told and instantly heard the clips lock into place. "Gee—thanks."

"It was nothing." He shrugged. "Need some help outside getting the skis on?"

"I think I can manage." Kathy was sure she'd be slipping and sliding all over the place, but she was too embarrassed to admit it. "Thank you anyway."

He shrugged and hoisted his skis up on his shoulder. "That's what I'm here for. If you need any help later, just look for me. O.K.?"

Kathy nodded. "Sure—see you later, Ken."

He smiled and began to walk away. "Your horse sure missed a great day for skiing," he called back to her over his shoulder.

"Yeah—just as well. You think *I* have trouble with the boots . . ."

Laughing, Ken shook his head. "See you later, Cowgirl."

After he'd left, Kathy gathered up her equipment and headed for the lesson area behind the lodge. The big heavy plastic boots were impossible to walk in. She felt like the Bride of Frankenstein clumping her way down the hill.

The group lessons were just about to begin. Kathy signed up and walked over to her assigned instructor, a tall, blond woman named Gretchen. Gretchen had a Swedish accent and looked as if she had been born wearing skis. She was a very patient teacher and cheerfully helped Kathy put her skis on before the class began.

Kathy lined up in a row with the other beginners, and they took turns doing the snowplow down a tiny beginner hill—otherwise known as the bunny slope. The idea was to keep the skis in a V shape, Gretchen explained, with the tips together and the back spread apart, which helped you control your speed. Of course Gretchen made it look easy, but practically everyone else in the class fell down immediately or zipped down the hill wildly, then fell. Practically everyone that is, except Kathy.

"Very good, Kathy. You have skied before?" Gretchen asked in her charming accent at the bottom of the first hill.

"Never. This is a total first," Kathy answered, feeling exhilarated from her short but exciting ride.

Gretchen laughed. "You did well. It's fun, isn't it?"

"Yeah!" Kathy nodded. She was surprised to realize that she was actually going to like skiing. "This is fun!"

After the snowplow, Gretchen taught the group S-turns—how to glide down the hill in a wide, zigzagging curve so that you didn't streak straight to the bottom totally out of control. Again, Kathy mastered the skill quickly. Once she was actually zigzagging down a hill, the skis and boots didn't feel as clumsy. The knack was shifting your weight from side to side, she discovered. A bit like surfing, or even skateboarding, which Kathy had been expert at back in California.

Once more Gretchen praised her progress. "I think

some of you are ready for the advanced group," she said, pointing to another group lesson on a larger hill nearby. She then called out Kathy's name and a few others. "Just tell the instructor I sent you over."

The next hill was considerably steeper, almost as big as the one Deena had skied off to earlier, Kathy noticed. She was scared at first and felt a knot in her stomach as she waited for her turn to ski down. The instructor—a guy named Skip who looked about college age to Kathy—led the group down the slope like a mother duck with its ducklings. He occasionally shouted instructions over his shoulder like "Head up! Stop looking at your skis!" Or "Big mogul! Get ready." And, most often, "Don't lean forward—sit down if you feel like you're falling."

Kathy had a few falls, but usually managed to right herself without help. Skip kept telling her she was "looking good," which was almost as encouraging as Gretchen's effusive praise. Finally Skip told Kathy and a few others that they were ready to ski on one of the advanced-beginner slopes.

Kathy jammed her poles in the snow and took a deep breath. It was almost eleven o'clock. Not only was she still in one piece, but she could actually make it down a respectable-sized hill without falling. This day wasn't going to be so bad after all, she thought as she skied toward the lift lines.

The base of the slope was very crowded. Shielding her eyes from the bright sunlight that bounced off the snow-covered mountain, Kathy searched for Deena. There were a lot of girls in powder-blue bib overalls with white headbands flying down the slope. Kathy waited near the end of the lift line a few minutes and hoped Deena would pass by. When she was moving around, Kathy had felt warm as toast. But now that she'd been standing still a few minutes, she was starting to feel the cold.

She decided to get in line and hope that she would meet Deena on the way down. Just as she maneuvered herself onto the end of the line, someone skied up beside her and came to an abrupt, stylish stop that sent up a spray of snow.

"Hey, Cowgirl. How are you doing?" It was Ken. He lifted his dark blue goggles, which were almost the same shade as his eyes.

"Pretty good. I didn't break anything yet."

"Come on, you're not so bad. I saw you coming down the slope in the lesson area before."

"You did?"

Ken nodded and got in line behind her. "You were O.K. Just remember not to look down at your ski tips. Keep your head up."

"That's what my instructor kept saying."

"There are a few basics you have to remember. And after that, skiing is really easy." Ken obviously adored skiing and adored talking about it, too. While they waited in line, he gave her a few more tips. Then he talked about the conditions on the higher slopes—the ones that looked to Kathy as if you had to get up there by helicopter.

When it was time to get on the lift, Ken and Kathy

were paired in the same gondola. She thought this was a lucky break, since she didn't exactly know how to get on and off. Like everything else that had to do with skiing, it was trickier than it looked.

Kathy sat back and enjoyed the ride. It was like being at an amusement park, she thought. As they glided over the treetops and trails, Ken told her about a ski trip he'd gone on with his family last winter to Vail, Colorado.

"You can't believe how great the powder is out there. It's dry, really fine powder," he said wistfully. "Not all grainy like here in New England. Did you ever hear the term corn snow?" Kathy shook her head. "That happens in the spring, when the snow melts and refreezes. It gets like little pieces of corn."

Kathy never realized that snow—slushy, fluffy, powdered, corny—could supply this much conversation. She had once heard that the Eskimo language had over a hundred words to describe different types of snow, and she thought Ken probably knew all of them. But she was glad he was so talkative, even if most of it was pretty boring. It calmed her nerves.

When the gondola reached the first station, Kathy prepared to get off. "This is my stop, I guess. Thanks for the lift," she joked.

"Don't get off here, Kathy," Ken said. "It's so crowded, you'll be bumping into yourself. Go up a little higher, to the next station," he suggested. "We'll go down together. I'll help you."

Kathy was apprehensive. Her instructor had said she was ready for an advanced-beginner slope—not the

Olympics. But by the time she thought it over, the chance to get off the lift had passed. Like it or not, she was stuck going up to the next station with Ken.

Just as Ken had predicted, it was far less crowded at the second stop on the lift. The trail was somewhat narrower and had more curves than Kathy had seen so far. But skiing near her, Ken warned her about the difficult stretches and told her what to do. Before Kathy knew it, the bottom of the slope was in sight again.

Kathy slowed down and came to a stop. She jammed her poles in the snow and loosened her scarf. She couldn't believe she had managed to get all the way down the hill, from the second lift station no less, without falling once. And she'd actually enjoyed it. Skimming around those tight curves had really been exciting.

Just ahead of her, Ken sped down the last stretch in perfect parallel form, his head bent and his poles tucked under his arms. When he noticed that she had stopped, he swung around in a huge arc and stopped short beside her, sending up another spray of snow.

"Nice skiing, Kathy. I thought I lost you on that last turn, but you hung in there like a pro."

"Thanks for warning me about the huge pothole. I could have killed myself skiing over that."

Ken smiled. "It's called a mogul."

"Whatever . . . I think we should tell somebody about that, so they can smooth it out."

"Smooth it out?" He chuckled. "They're put there on purpose, to make the trail more interesting. It wouldn't be any fun if it was flat as an ironing board."

"Oh, sure," Kathy said skeptically. "I guess not."

"Ready for another run?"

Kathy was ready for some hot chocolate. But it was fun to ski with Ken, almost like having a private instructor.

"O.K., let's go." Kathy slipped her poles back over her wrists and led the way over to the lift line. One more run with Captain Mogul, Kathy thought, and I'll really look like I know what I'm doing when I meet up with Deena.

Chapter 3

Deena was honestly worried about Kathy. It was after twelve o'clock, and she hadn't seen her all morning. She had skied over to the beginner slope, suspecting that Kathy wasn't nearly as experienced as she had claimed. But to Deena's surprise, Kathy hadn't been there. Deena had checked other likely trails for Kathy too. She had even taken a look inside the lodge, worried that Kathy might have hurt herself.

It was her fault for being in such a rush this morning. She should have waited for Kathy, even though she was not as good a skier and would have cramped Deena's style. They could have skied together for some of the morning, Deena thought. She had just been too concerned that Ken might see her on the bunny slope and think she was a beginner, too.

Well, I'll make it up to her later, Deena promised herself. We'll ski together the whole afternoon. Maybe I can even teach her a few things—if she'll let me.

Deena had no sooner finished the thought than she spotted Kathy. First she felt relieved. Kathy was not in the infirmary with an ice pack pressed on something sprained, as she had feared. Then she was shocked. Kathy was in line with Ken Buckly, talking and fooling around as if he were an old friend.

Deena felt a sharp twinge of envy. Ken had paid some extra attention to Kathy before they had boarded the bus, she recalled. But Deena had seen boys act like that with Kathy before. She seemed to bring out the wise-cracking side of them. Even a really mature guy like Ken. It didn't mean anything, Deena assured herself as she skied toward them. Her cousin was Ken's complete and total opposite. He could never be interested in someone as wild as Kathy. The idea was too outrageous. They had probably met up in line by accident, and he was just trying to be nice by talking to her.

Deena skied up to them in line and came to an impressive stop. "Hi, guys," she said brightly.

Ken was the first one to notice her. He was wearing Kathy's cowboy hat. "Hi, Deena. Having a good day?"

Deena felt a knot tighten in her stomach. But she kept smiling. "A great day. I haven't stopped once since we got here—except to look around for you, Kath," she added. "Where have you been?"

Kathy just shrugged. She couldn't very well admit that

26

she'd been taking a lesson for most of the morning. "Uh—Ken and I went down the blue trail for a while."

Deena swallowed hard. Here she was worried about Kathy, and she'd been having a fine time all morning—with Ken! The blue trail was the intermediate slope. Deena had never suspected that Kathy was quite that good on skis. This was turning out to be a day full of surprises.

"Did you guys have a good run?" she asked lightly, glancing over at Ken.

"It was fun," Ken said. "I haven't been on that trail in awhile."

"Of course not—I'm sure you always ski the red trails, Ken." Deena tucked a strand of hair under her headband and smiled at him. "I was just heading over to the lift for Jackknife Peak," she said, mentioning the most difficult slope at the resort. "Have you tried it yet today?"

"Not yet—I was meaning to go over there when I met up with Kathy. I heard the conditions are just super on top."

"Why don't you come with me?" Deena asked, ignoring Kathy's suddenly indignant expression. She had wanted to spend some time with Kathy. But after hearing that Kathy had been skiing for hours with Ken, Deena couldn't stop herself. She was seeing red.

Ken shrugged. "Sure—let's go." He took off Kathy's hat and dropped it back on her head. "Happy trails, partner."

"Wait!" The hat dropped down over Kathy's eyes and she pushed it back up. "I'll come with you guys."

"No offense, Kath—but I think Jackknife is too advanced for you," Deena said. "When Ken and I are done, I'll meet you back here and we'll have lunch."

Kathy wondered if Deena was telling the truth, or just exaggerating to make herself look like such a super skier. What the heck—the blue trail she had just gone down with Ken hadn't been that tough. How much harder could a red trail be? Besides, she didn't want to ski alone. So she fell a few times. Big deal. She wasn't afraid of that anymore. It was cold and wet, but it wasn't life-threatening, as she had thought this morning.

"I'm coming, too, Deena," she insisted. "I'll be fine . . . won't I, Ken?"

"Uh—sure. As long as you take it easy and don't go down too fast. You know what they say, 'No guts, no glory.' "

Hearing Ken encourage Kathy made Deena even angrier. She pulled down her goggles and pushed off on her skis. "Well, let's get going then," she said.

Once they reached the peak, she was sure Kathy would be petrified and choose to take the lift back down. She predicted it would be a case of "Better safe than sorry' for her supposedly gutsy cousin.

Kathy didn't understand what Deena was in such a snit about. Hadn't she said that she wanted them to have fun skiing together today? And didn't she want her to get to know a few of her preppie friends? Wasn't that exactly what was going on? Kathy just didn't understand Deena sometimes—*most* of the time, actually.

Brooding on these thoughts, Kathy got into the gondola with Ken and Deena. The lift for Jackknife Peak had larger cars that could hold four people. Deena sat next to Ken, and Kathy sat across from them. Their conversation was more talk about snow, and she certainly didn't have anything to add.

The lift was taking them higher and higher. The lodge was beginning to look like a miniature log cabin in one of those paperweights that had snowflakes swirling around inside it, Kathy thought. They even traveled through a cloud and came out the other end.

"Hey—that cloud was really neat," Kathy said, interrupting Ken and Deena's conversation.

"It reminds me of a poem by Carl Sandburg," Deena said to Ken. "'The fog comes on little cat feet...'" she recited in a gentle voice.

"It reminds me of a song by the Pinheads," Kathy said, "'I just can't evacuate this toxic cloud of love...'" Kathy sang with feeling, her eyes squeezed shut.

"I don't think I ever heard of the Pinheads," Ken said.

"No great loss," Deena said lightly. She knew Ken played the French horn and must prefer *real* music. He probably thought Kathy looked and sounded ridiculous singing that trash.

"They're a new group from England. Really hot," Kathy said, ignoring Deena's barb. "Some people just don't have any taste in music, know what I mean?"

Before Ken had a chance to reply, the gondola swung up to the platform, and they hurriedly unloaded. When they reached the starting point of the trail, Kathy looked down and felt her stomach do a backflip. She couldn't believe how high they were. She was about to say something to Deena, but noticed her cousin's I-told-you-so look. Kathy wasn't going to give Deena the satisfaction of admitting she had been right.

"Ready?" Deena asked her.

"Sure," Kathy shrugged, and pulled her scarf tighter.

"Why don't you go first, Kathy," Ken suggested, "and we'll follow. That way I'll be right behind you in case you have any trouble."

"O.K." Kathy nodded and got her skis into the right position to begin. She felt nervous going first, but she figured Ken would shout out some tips and warnings to help her down the slope, as he had the last time. "Here goes nothing." Kathy swallowed hard and pushed off.

"See you at the bottom," Deena called, expertly launching herself close behind Kathy.

It wasn't so bad, Kathy thought at first. Not much more difficult than the trail she'd gone down with Ken. Then all of a sudden the trail became much narrower and steeper. Kathy heard Ken and Deena shouting to her, but she couldn't understand a word they said. She glanced back over her shoulder, but taking her eyes off the trail for a second nearly caused her to ski right off the mountain. She tried to remember what Ken and her instructors had said about looking up, and sitting down, and pushing out with her feet.

30

But she was going faster and faster, zooming down the mountain like a runaway train. She couldn't remember anything she had learned about slowing down or stopping; her mind was blank.

She flew past a few other skiers, narrowly missing a head-on collision. They shouted and waved their arms at her, but Kathy was moving so fast it was all a blur.

The trail, which had so far been straight, took a sudden dip and then a sharp curve. Kathy wanted to cover her eyes with her hands, but she knew she'd kill herself for sure. Suddenly she was airborne, and a pole flew out of her hand. When her skis touched ground again, she was tilted crazily off-balance. She slid on one ski for a few yards, the other leg up in the air. Then she fell altogether, tumbling downhill for what seemed like a very long time.

She opened her eyes for an instant, long enough to see that she was aimed head first for a cluster of huge bushes. With her eyes closed she felt herself sink into the branches. It was a moment before she realized she had finally stopped moving. But when she tried to get up, she was stuck. Each attempt to free herself caused another pile of snow to come loose from the branches and fall on her head and back.

"Kathy—can you hear me?" she heard Ken calling her.

Kathy tried to answer, but had to first spit out a mouthful of snow before she could speak. "I'm stuck! Get me out of here!"

"Kathy!" It was Deena, sounding hysterical. "Are you hurt? Can you breathe under there?"

Kathy started wiggling again, determined this time to get herself free. Stuck head-first in a bush! This was just too mortifying to be true.

"No—don't move around like that, Kathy! Something might be broken," Deena told her.

"Stop playing Florence Nightingale, Deena, and just help me out of this bush!" Kathy sputtered as she thrashed around.

Convinced that Kathy was actually alive and kicking under there, Ken and Deena began pulling away the branches.

Kathy shakily came to a sitting position. She was covered with snow from head to foot. She could feel it, cold and icy in her ears and stuck to her eyelashes, down the the back of her sweater and in the waistband of her jeans. Right through the seat of her pants actually. With a jolt, she realized the back of her pants had split.

She felt like crying—not because anything hurt, but because she was so embarrassed.

"You're sure nothing hurts?" Ken said, crouching down beside here. He gently flicked a clump of snow off her shoulder. "Maybe I should get the ski patrol to pick you up, just in case."

"I don't need the ski patrol. I'm fine," Kathy insisted. Her spiky layered haircut was standing out in all directions, like the branch of a snow-covered pine tree.

"Don't try to get up too fast," Deena said, crouching down on the other side. Poor Kathy looked like such a mess, Deena really felt sorry for her. It was a miracle she hadn't broken every bone in her body after that fall.

There was a tiny scratch on her chin, but otherwise, she really looked fine.

Well, actually, she looked pretty funny. Now that she knew Kathy wasn't hurt, Deena had to struggle not to laugh. It had been a little depressing to watch Kathy take to skiing so easily. Deena had had to work hard before she was able to ski this trail. She was sorry that Kathy had taken such a bad spill. But in a way it would teach her a lesson. She couldn't just breeze in and be an instant expert at anything she tried.

"Want some tissues?" Deena asked, patting Kathy's shoulder.

"Thanks." Kathy took the entire package and mopped off her face. Leave it to Deena—always prepared. She wondered if her cousin had a paper bag handy that she could wear over her head. "Oh, my God—I'm bleeding!" she gasped, looking down at the wad of tissues.

"It's just a scratch," Deena assured her.

"Where? Let's see," Ken said, sounding alarmed. He knelt down again beside Kathy, and Deena nearly groaned out loud when he put his hand on Kathy's chin to examine the cut. "It's nothing," he said finally. "But I think we'd better take you down to the infirmary anyway. You might have sprained something without knowing it."

"O.K. Let's go," Kathy said, amazingly agreeable for once, Deena noticed.

Ken helped Kathy up. Her legs felt wobbly, and she leaned on his arm for support. Deena quickly got on the other side, though Kathy didn't seem to notice her.

They made it down the hill to the infirmary. Luckily, Kathy's sweater covered the split in her pants. A doctor was able to examine Kathy right away. She quickly confirmed that Kathy was still in one piece and definitely going to survive. After swabbing some disinfectant on her scratch, the doctor suggested a hot bath that night, followed by some aspirin for any bumps or bruises that might turn up later.

"Ask your boyfriend to go back up the hill and get your skis," she said, pointing to Ken, who was standing with Deena nearby. "I think you've seen enough snow for one day."

"Uh—he's not my boyfriend," Kathy said to the doctor. "Just a friend."

"I'll pick them up for you, Kathy. No problem," Ken said.

Deena nervously twisted her gloves around in her hands. She glanced at Ken. He was blushing! Was he really getting a crush on Kathy? Or was he just so conscientious about his role as the ski club president that he felt responsible for her?

"I'll go back up with you, Ken," Deena said. "Maybe we could have one more run—if it's O.K. with you, Kathy?"

She really didn't want to spend the rest of the day holding Kathy's hand. But she had to ask. She hoped Kathy would refuse and give her some time alone with Ken. She let out a soft sigh of relief at Kathy's reply.

"No—you guys keep skiing. I'll be fine, honest." Kathy felt like crawling into a hole. She just wanted to be

34

alone for a while. If Roy were around, he could cheer her up. But she didn't feel like being with Deena and Ken.

Finally she was able to convince them to go back outside and continue skiing. Once they had gone, Kathy got a needle and thread from the nurse in the infirmary, went behind a curtain, and started to sew up her jeans.

It never failed: whenever she let Deena talk her into something, it was a disaster. This was absolutely the last time she would ever let Deena talk her into doing something healthy out in the fresh air. This *healthy* stuff could finish a person for good.

Chapter 4

"All right, crew, we're down to the wire. Less than two weeks until our Grand Opening. If we're going to make it, we really have to dig in our heels and work," Deena's mother said with a sigh. "Just look at this list."

It was Sunday morning, the day after the ski trip, and everyone was finishing up breakfast. Seated at the head of the kitchen table, Lydia Scott frowned down at her long computerized printout. Deena admired the way her mother was always so organized. She had a natural flair for keeping track of their progress and deciding what jobs were more urgent than others. Deena knew that if it wasn't for her mother, they would never have gotten even this far on the refurbishing of the inn.

Yet, while Lydia was the organization behind the project, it was Kathy's mother, Nancy, who always came up with creative ideas. She came up with schemes for the painting and decorating of the rooms, and the refinishing of old furniture. Some of them were actually too wild to be believed. But keeping to a schedule was really not her "thing," as she would explain in her sixties slang. Nevertheless, the sisters' styles complemented each other. And working with their children, they had made great progress in fixing up the rambling old Victorian-style hotel.

But somehow, the more they did, the more work there seemed to be. Refurbishing the inn was a mammoth project, and lately Deena got the feeling that if their mothers had realized how much effort and expense it would take, they might never have decided to attempt it.

"What can Kathy and I do today, Mom?" Deena said, volunteering both herself and her cousin. Kathy had been unusually quiet this morning at the breakfast table. Probably still pouting over her disastrous ski trip, Deena thought. But now she picked her head up from the Sunday comics and gave Deena a look.

"There's so much on the list. Take your pick. You girls can rip down the wallpaper in the second-floor bathroom. And after that, help me hang those curtains we made for the guest rooms up there." She made a few marks on her list, then sighed again. "I don't know how we'll ever get all of this done by Thanksgiving, Nancy. Maybe we should postpone."

Kathy's mother poured herself another cup of coffee.

"It will all get done in time, you'll see," she assured her sister. "Just go with the flow. These things have a way of falling into place," Nancy added with a smile and a vague wave of her hand.

"Nan—the only thing that's going with the flow and falling into place around here is the roof. The patch right over our fanciest guest room, to be exact. What are we going to do about that?"

"Call someone, I guess," Nancy said. "But it will probably cost a lot to fix it. Too bad we can't do it ourselves."

"Neat!" Johnny, Kathy's nine-year-old brother, was instantly excited at the prospect of walking around up on the roof. "I'll help. I don't even need a ladder. I can go out the attic window, even though you guys are probably too big to fit, and—"

"Don't even think about it, buddy," Nancy told her son.

"Besides, we need you for more important jobs," Lydia said. "How about helping me clean out those last two rooms on the second floor today? There's a lot of junk to haul away. I need some muscle."

"Sure, Aunt Lydia," Johnny replied, sounding a bit downcast about missing out on the roof adventure.

"And I'll keep painting," Nancy said. "I mixed the most gorgeous shade of peach for that last second-floor bedroom, Lydia. It's totally delicious."

It was Kathy and Deena's turn to clear up the kitchen. Deena piled up some plates, sticky with syrup and French toast crusts, and carried them to the sink. She could never get used to her aunt's excitement over just mixing a new color of paint. Her mother never bubbled like that, but her aunt really sounded like a kid sometimes, Deena thought, and it was usually fun.

Now, dressed in her bathrobe, with her big coffee mug in hand, Nancy took her spattered painting cap off the counter and pulled it on. "Okay, I'm psyched. We each have our jobs for the day. Let's put some hustle in those bustles, guys."

Lydia smiled and got up from her chair. She was wearing a flannel shirt and corduroy jeans, her blond hair covered by a blue bandanna. "My thought exactly . . . well, *almost* exactly."

Kathy and Deena cleaned up the kitchen quickly, then went down to the basement for the tools they needed to tear down the bathroom wallpaper.

"This is not as easy as it looks," Kathy said, after tearing off her first strip. "Look, about half of it just sticks there. It looks like it melted onto the wall or something."

"You have to put some of the wallpaper solvent on it, then use the scraper," Deena explained as she set up the ladder. Not even Kathy could put her in a bad mood today. Ken had not been far from her thoughts all morning. She kept thinking about the time they had spent skiing together yesterday afternoon, after Kathy's fortuitous fall. They'd really had fun. She decided that Ken didn't have a crush on Kathy after all. How could he? Kathy was his complete opposite—the idea was just absurd. He was only being nice to her because he was the head of the ski club. That's the kind of guy Ken was, which was why Deena liked him so much.

Deena thought now it had actually been lucky that Ken and Kathy had skied down the intermediate slope together. She knew she would have never gotten up the nerve to talk to him otherwise. Now she felt as if they were actually friends. And, she hoped, they'd soon be more than that—but first things first, she cautioned herself. She was going to join the ski club next week, and she would get to see Ken at the meetings and on all the ski trips. They really had so much in common. Not only skiing. Deena just had this feeling that once he got to know her, he'd see that they were a perfect match. She could hardly wait for the day to be over so that she could see him at school on Monday.

Deena felt so happy and lighthearted, as if she could float up to the ceiling without using the ladder at all. "It's not so bad," she told Kathy as she yanked off a big piece. Dust flew in her face and she coughed.

"Are you kidding? This is going to take us all day," Kathy grumbled, grabbing the bottle of solvent and a scraper.

"Hey—don't stand on the edge of the bathtub like that!" Deena turned to see her cousin, who precariously balanced on the edge of the clawfoot tub, scraping at a stubborn scrap of paper. "There's no snow to dig you out of in here, Kathy. Haven't you noticed? Or didn't you learn your lesson yesterday?"

Kathy stopped scraping and glared at her. "Yes, I learned my lesson, Deena." It was amazing to Deena how well Kathy could mimic her. "Which was, never, ever, under any circumstances whatsoever, let

40

you talk me into anything that you think will 'enrich' my trashy little, uncultured life. That was the lesson I learned."

Deena shrugged and attacked another section of the wall with vigor. She had talked Kathy into the trip with the best intentions. But somehow, as things usually did where Kathy was concerned, her best intentions had backfired.

"You said you knew how to ski."

"I do know how to ski," Kathy insisted. She'd been humiliated enough yesterday. She wasn't going to admit to Deena that she had been faking it from the start. Deena would never let her hear the end of it. She hopped lightly from the edge of the bathtub onto the toilet seat cover. "I just never skied down Mount Everest before, that's all."

"Well, don't say I didn't try to warn you. Of course, you wouldn't listen to me." Deena splashed some solvent on the wall and heard Kathy grumble something unintelligible in response. "Poor Ken was quite upset for the rest of the afternoon. He kept saying that he shouldn't have encouraged you to try Jackknife." Deena felt a secret thrill just saying his name out loud. "But that's the way Ken is, serious and responsible." Not like Roy, she restrained herself from adding. "I told him it wouldn't have made one bit of difference if he had encouraged you or not, because you never listen to anybody."

"Thanks, Deena." Kathy tossed a big wet sponge into the sink. "I can always count on you for good publicity."

"Well, you never listen to anything I say, that's for

sure." Deena sighed. The way that Kathy always put her ideas and opinions down hurt her feelings more than Kathy knew. She just knew more about some things than Kathy did. Was that a crime? Kathy was so stubborn, she refused to give her credit for anything.

"The only thing I feel like listening to right now is some music. No offense. I'm going to get the tape player. Be right back." Kathy wiped off her hands and stomped out of the bathroom.

So Deena was better on skis. Big deal. Kathy was sure that by tomorrow afternoon, everyone in school was going to know that she'd been a total klutz and had to be helped down from the mountain. Deena would make sure they heard every last detail. She certainly didn't feel like spending the rest of the day talking about it, just so Deena could gloat.

She picked up the tape player and some tapes. A few minutes of Nuclear Waste at high volume would put a lid on Deena for sure.

The girls passed the rest of the day scraping off wallpaper and arguing over what kind of music to put on the tape player. Finally Deena's mother negotiated a compromise. They took turns, each playing one side of a tape of their choice. The selections throughout the afternoon seesawed between tapes like *Greatest Heavy Metal Hits of the Decade* and *Swan Lake.*

* * *

The next day at school Kathy met her friends in the cafeteria at their usual table. "Hey, Manelli," Roy

42

greeted her through a mouthful of sandwich. "How did the home improvements go yesterday?"

Roy had called yesterday morning to see if she wanted to take a ride into town on his motorcycle, but she had explained that she had to help out at the inn.

"Scraping wallpaper is so-o-o boring. I thought I was going to nod off and fall into the bathtub. Especially when Deena put her dumb classical music on."

Roy laughed. "I love scraping wallpaper. It's the greatest."

Kathy looked at him wide-eyed. "You're kidding, right?"

"But not nearly as much fun as plumbing. Now, fixing a leaky faucet, that to me is a real trip."

Kathy turned to her friend Ellecia. "He fell off his bike and hit his head, right?"

"He's weird. Haven't you noticed?" Ellecia said.

Tilting her head back, Zee, Ellecia's friend, peered at Kathy from under a fringe of spiky, blue and magenta streaked bangs. "Yeah, we are talking *major* weirdness ... bless his pointed little head."

Roy laughed even harder. "No, listen. I'm serious. The other day I got this idea on how to make some extra money. I'm going to hire myself out to do odd jobs that other people hate, or just don't know how to do. I'm going to put up some signs in town and maybe take an ad in the paper. Meet Mr. Fix-it, guys. What do you think?"

"You're a regular ... gee, what was that word Ms. Barlow was talking about in economics today?" Ellecia chomped on a big wad of gum and made a few snapping sounds. "Oh, yeah . . . a regular auntrepinner, Roy."

"Entrepreneur, you mean," Kathy said, correcting her. Ellecia was a good friend, but a little loosely wrapped in the brains department. She did have really neat clothes, though. Her parents were divorced, and whenever she went to visit her father in New York, she bought loads of great stuff down in Soho and Chelsea. Kathy was dying for a pair of patent-leather oxfords, just like Ellecia's. But she knew she'd never find them up here in the backwoods.

Aside from Ellecia's wardrobe, Kathy was thinking that her mother and aunt could really use Roy's help at the inn. Although the entire family had worked hard all day Sunday, there were still so many things to be fixed. They would never get it all done in time. Many of the repair jobs were really too complicated for them to try on their own—like the leaky roof—and so expensive that they kept putting off hiring somebody.

Roy would be the perfect solution to the problem. But would they hire him? They didn't like him—which Kathy could never understand since he was really so sweet and thoughtful. The problem was that Roy had made a bad first impression on her mother and aunt, and Deena hadn't helped matters. It all started when Kathy had begun dating Roy in September. She wasn't allowed to ride on his motorcycle, and once when she did, Deena ratted on her. Her mother even forbade her to see Roy at all for a while.

Everything was finally smoothed out, but Kathy knew

44

they still didn't like him. All they talked about was how tough and unruly he *looked*. Especially Aunt Lydia, who thought that just because he wore a leather jacket and rode a motorcycle, he was an aspiring criminal or something. And Deena's wisecracks about him just added fuel to the fire.

Her mother was a little better, but not much. If she had some reservations about Roy, she was wise enough to keep them to herself. But Kathy had a feeling that even she wasn't crazy about him.

Kathy unwrapped a sandwich she had brought from home and decided not to tell Roy that there was so much work to be done at the inn. Why get his hopes up? Maybe as their opening day got closer, her mother and aunt would get desperate enough to call him.

"I think it's a great idea, Roy. You're always real handy fixing your bike," was all she said.

"Sure I am. A friend of mine works at the hardware store in town, and I can get all my supplies at a discount. I'm going to put a stack of fliers in there, near the door and by the check-out. Think I can borrow that set of colored markers you have, Kathy?"

"Sure—I can help you do the lettering if you want." Kathy knew Roy was embarrassed to ask her to help him. But if he did the lettering all alone, the signs would really look like a mess. Nobody would call him.

"Great! I'll come by tonight, after supper."

"O.K." Kathy took a sip of her apple juice. "That should be fine."

"O.K., I've got to get going. Got to study for a math

45

quiz, next period. Geometry is the pits, know what I mean?" He crumpled up his lunch bag into a tight ball and tossed it into a nearby garbage can. "Two points, all right! See you."

As Roy dashed off, Kathy realized that since they'd ended up talking about his Mr. Fix-it plans, nobody had mentioned Saturday's ski trip. Her friends had probably already heard how she'd wrapped herself around that bush. It was really kind of funny when you thought about it, Kathy reflected.

As if reading her thoughts, Ellecia said, "So how was that ski trip, Kathy?"

"I heard you had a head-on with a tree," Zee added.

"It was a bush. A big bush," Kathy said, crumbling up her lunch bag. "*Not* a tree. Who told you a tree? Deena, I bet."

"I just heard it around. You know." Zee played with one of her long hanging earrings, which was made out of strands of colored telephone wire and strung with sequins.

"I wouldn't get on a pair of skis for anything. I mean, I just don't get it. Flopping around in all that snow." Ellecia shivered.

"All these prepped-out kids around here really get off on stuff like that," Zee said. "Tennis and swim team—I mean, could you barf, or what?"

Ellecia agreed. "Alice once wanted me to take tennis lessons." Alice was Ellecia's mother, whom Ellecia always referred to by her first name. "But I said, 'Like Alice, I mean, what's the *concept* here?' " She shrugged one

46

skinny shoulder under her baggy black sweater. "It's the same with skiing."

"Yeah, well, I can wait until my next incarnation before I try it again. That's for sure," Kathy stated.

"Come on, Cowgirl, you don't mean that," said a voice behind her.

Kathy turned around to see Ken standing with his arms crossed. He had probably overheard their conversation. He smiled at Kathy and sat down.

"In all the Westerns I ever saw, if the horse kicks you off, you're supposed to shake off the dust and get right back on."

"Yeah, well..." Kathy didn't know what to say. On top of being a grade-A klutz, now the guy thought she had no spunk. "Maybe after a few more hot baths I'll feel differently about it."

"You weren't really hurt, though, were you?" Ken asked, seeming concerned.

Kathy shook her head. "But I wish I could have seen an instant replay of myself. I must have looked like I was breaking every bone in my body."

"I hope that fall doesn't keep you from skiing, Kathy," Ken said seriously. "When I was first learning, I took much worse falls than yours, honest. I remember coming down a hill out of control one time and yelling my head off because I couldn't stop. I could see people at the bottom of the slope trying to run out of the way, like in a Charlie Chaplin movie—first to one side, then the next. Mothers were grabbing their children and running for their lives!"

Kathy and Ellecia were both laughing hard.

"I'm talking about Olympic-class falling here. Your little spill was nothing to brag about."

Kathy smiled. "Thanks, Ken. That makes me feel better," she admitted.

"Feel better, nothing. You're a natural on skis, and pretty gutsy to even try that last slope." He smiled at her and shook his head. "I shouldn't have let you go up, but—"

"Hey, don't be silly," Kathy said. "I knew what I was doing. Or rather, I *didn't* know."

Ken laughed. "Well, maybe I can make it up to you. I have this great how-to video for skiing. Do you have a VCR?"

"Uh-huh," Kathy nodded. Her mother and aunt had bought one last week. It was a big expense, but they had decided that guests would expect the inn to have one.

"What if I bring the tape over sometime and give you a few pointers?" Ken said.

"Uh—sure." Ken's suggestion came as such a surprise, Kathy didn't know what to say. "That would be fun, I guess."

"Great. And think of it this way, Kathy: how much damage can you do in your own living room?" He stood up and pushed up the sleeves on his yellow crew-neck sweater. In his ski coverall on Saturday, Kathy hadn't noticed Ken's muscular arms. Maybe he was a preppie, but he was no wimp. "See you later," he said.

"See you," Kathy said.

Ellecia sat staring off into space, chewing her gum like a mesmerized cow. "I can't believe you just made a date with that guy, Kath," she said finally.

"Really, Kathy," Zee said.

Kathy could hardly believe it herself. "It's not a real date," she insisted. "He's just a nice guy. I think he wants to be friends."

"Right," Ellecia said dryly. "I'll tell you one thing, I'm starting to get the concept of skiing. I mean, he's really cute."

"You think so?" Kathy, too, was starting to think Ken was pretty cute. He really went out of his way to be nice to her, and he certainly didn't have to. He was so popular, and she was just an outer-fringe newcomer at school. She would not have readily admitted these thoughts to Ellecia, however, and was surprised to hear the envy in her friend's voice.

"Definitely," Ellecia snapped her gum in an irrefutable manner. "That sweater was gross, though. He'd look great in black leather, don't you think?"

"For sure," Zee agreed. She vigorously nodded her head, causing her sequined earrings to fly in all directions.

"I don't know. I didn't think his sweater was that bad," Kathy said. That was one thing about Ellecia's fashion sense that Kathy didn't agree with. Ellecia thought the entire universe would be improved by more black leather. Ken was just fine the way he was, she thought. He wasn't her usual type—not at all like Roy.

But that was like comparing apple pie with a chili dog—
Roy definitely being the chili dog, with the works. Which
was better?

It all depended on what you were in the mood for, Kathy decided, feeling pleased with herself for having been
asked on a date—as unbelievable as that sounded—by
Ken Buckly.

Maybe Deena was right after all. Maybe it would be
good to make a few friends in the mainstream of the
school. Ken was the perfect place to start if she wanted to
make some friends in the school's most popular circles.

Kathy sipped the rest of her apple juice, feeling happy
inside about Ken. As her friend might say, Kathy was
starting to "get the concept" about Ken Buckly.

Chapter 5

"Hi, Deena. How are you doing today?" Ken gave Deena a cheerful greeting and a big smile when she swung open the inn's heavy front door.

Face to face with Ken, Deena was speechless. She could barely breathe, much less remember to say hello and step out of the way so he could come inside.

She had expected the doorbell to be Mr. Krupshaw, the roofer, coming to look over the leak. When she recognized Ken through the front door's panel of frosted glass, Deena thought she was going to faint.

She'd been thinking about Ken all day in school, and had even written a poem about him during study hall. She had tried to run into him in the hallways and cafeteria without any luck at all. And here he was, standing right in front of her, ringing her very own doorbell. This was too wonderful to be believed!

"Ken—hi. What a nice surprise," Deena said breathlessly. She stepped aside so he could come in. It was kismet—destiny, Deena was convinced. Her thoughts had drawn him here, like magnetic waves. "I, uh, thought I would see you in school today . . . but I guess we missed each other."

"I guess so," Ken said. He looked around the inn's big front hallway with curiosity. "Gee—this is some place. I've never been inside before."

"It's neat, isn't it? We're planning our Grand Opening for Thanksgiving weekend. It's going to be really fun." Deena almost asked him then if he wanted to come to the party, but quickly got hold of herself. She didn't want to seem overanxious. And Ken was probably the kind of guy who liked it if you played it a little cool, she mused.

She fleetingly wished he had given her some warning. She'd been exercising and was not exactly dressed to receive guests. She was wearing a pink sweat shirt, gray shorts with blue exercise tights underneath, and thick yellow socks that flopped over the top of her white aerobics shoes. Her hair was tied back in a scraggly ponytail. Even though she knew he admired the athletic type, she hoped he didn't think she looked like a sweaty mess.

"I was just in the middle of my exercise routine," she explained. "I do some low-impact aerobics and a lot of ballet stretches. I took classical dance classes for years," she said, hoping he would be impressed. "I find the warm-up routine for ballet is a really wonderful warm-up for skiing. Did you ever try it?"

"Uh—no." Ken looked puzzled. "I play basketball. It's a real good workout."

"Even football players take ballet classes. Didn't you ever read about that?"

"Uh—no." Ken crossed his arms over his chest. "I wrestle and run cross-country in the fall. Football is not for me."

"I don't like football, either," Deena said. "It's too violent. It's not just the sport that offends me, it's the whole mind-set, the political implications and all."

She glanced over at Ken. He gave her a thoughtful look and nodded. "If I had gone out for football, I couldn't have been president of the ski club this year."

"Really? I'm glad you chose the ski club. I'm going to join at the next meeting, and I was thinking that I could teach everyone these great stretching exercises. You don't really need a barre. You can just rest your ankle on the stairs, like this," she demonstrated, placing the heel of her foot on the fourth step, arching her arms overhead and then lunging forward. "It's perfect for warming up your hamstrings. See what I mean?"

Deena was sure that Ken would be impressed by her grace and athletic ability. When she glanced over at him, he looked awestruck, but something told her it was not quite the reaction she had intended.

"Hey, that's great. I think I'll try it sometime—listen, I don't want to interrupt your workout, Deena. Is Kathy around?"

"Kathy?" Deena stood up and faced Ken. "I think she's upstairs."

"Great—I brought this video over for her, to help her with her skiing." He showed Deena the black plastic case of the video cassette. "She told me in school today that it would be O.K. if I dropped by with it."

"Oh." Deena felt as if the floor had just dropped out from under her. She was crushed and mortified. Ken wasn't here to see her at all. He was here to see Kathy!

Deena's mind was racing. He must think I'm a total jerk, talking to him all this time when he came to see Kathy. I've made an absolute fool of myself. Now he'll know for sure how much I like him! This is a nightmare!

But she managed enough poise to say, "Kathy's upstairs. I'll go get her for you. Why don't you wait in the living room? I have to go finish my routine. I really hate to cool down right in the middle," she called to him as she ran up the stairs.

Up in the third-floor room she and her cousin shared, Deena found Kathy, sprawled out on her unmade bed, atop most of the clothes she'd worn for the past week. A copy of *A Tale of Two Cities* was propped on her stomach, and she was singing along loudly to a tape on her Walkman. She didn't even notice Deena standing in the doorway. "O-o-oh, O-o-oh, baby," she wailed loudly. "My soul is in a vise. Why can't you be nice? You're like a chunk of ice . . . "

Did she have to sing so loudly all the time? She sounded like a heartbroken hound, Deena thought. Kathy's singing was doubly annoying to her at this moment.

54

"Kathy, someone is downstairs to see you," Deena announced from the doorway, her arms folded over her chest.

Kathy just kept singing, "O-o-oh honey. I just can't last the night. You're a piece of kryptonite. And I'm too weak to fight . . . "

"Kathy!" Deena stepped over to the bed and pulled off Kathy's earphones. "Didn't you hear me? I said someone is here to see you!"

Startled, Kathy sat up and stared at Deena as if she'd gone berserk. "What's the matter with you? Why are you shouting at me?"

"I'm shouting because you didn't hear me the first five hundred times, that's all," Deena grumbled. She turned her back on Kathy and began straightening up her already orderly desktop. "I think you really should ask yourself why you have to shut out reality by plugging yourself into that machine all the time."

"Simple, I like to listen to music. Also, I don't have to hear people shouting at me for no reason." Kathy stood up and straightened out her oversized blue sweater. "I thought Roy said he was coming over after supper," she said more to herself than Deena. "I have to read this book for a test tomorrow. I was just starting to concentrate."

As if anyone could call that ridiculous behavior studying! Deena thought. "It's not Roy—it's Ken Buckly."

"Ken? Gee . . . " Kathy found a comb in the pile of junk on her nighttable and ran it through her thick brown hair. "Has he been down there long?"

"A few minutes. Not long," Deena said curtly, with her back still turned.

She was glad her cousin couldn't see her expression. The unmistakable note of excitement in Kathy's voice stung Deena sharply. So Kathy really liked him, too. *Boyscout* type, and all. Deena sighed and shuffled the books on her desk from one side to the other. She'd heard the old expression "Opposites attract," but she hadn't realized it applied to life forms from different planets!

As Deena mulled over her painful thoughts, Kathy hurriedly fixed her hair, put on some lip gloss and a pair of big hanging earrings that looked like bunches of bananas. In a flash she was out of the room and flying down the stairs.

Deena tried to do some school work. But she couldn't help thinking about Kathy and Ken downstairs in the living room. She was shocked and couldn't quite believe it. Another part of her felt hurt, even betrayed. The fact that Kathy really didn't know she liked Ken seemed irrelevant. And still another part of her felt awfully foolish. If they actually started seeing each other, how was she ever going to live with Kathy in the same house? Wasn't it *already* difficult enough?

Deena got up from her desk and paced around the bedroom. The jeans, sweater, and scarf Kathy had worn skiing on Saturday were still in a pile on the floor, and Deena gave them a good kick, sending them flying.

She knew that no matter *what*, she wasn't going to let Kathy know that she liked Ken, too. Kathy must never ever find out her secret. After all, she still had her pride.

The phone rang and Deena collected herself and answered it. She hoped it was one of her friends, but when she picked up she recognized Roy's voice on the other end.

"Hi, Deena, is Kathy around?"

"Uh—hi, Roy. Sure, she's here . . . but she can't come to the phone right now . . . "

Deena didn't know what to say. She was almost positive that Kathy wouldn't want Roy to know that she was getting private ski lessons from Ken Buckly. Then she felt annoyed. Why was *she* worrying about Kathy's love life! At this very moment, in her own living room, Kathy was destroying all her hopes and dreams about Ken. And did she worry for one little second about Deena's life? Guess again!

" . . . so I was supposed to come by after supper. But now I have to stay home and watch my monsterette little sister while my parents go shopping." Roy had been explaining something, and Deena had hardly heard a word of it. "So I have to come over and get the markers now."

"You're coming here? Now?"

"Are you feeling O.K., Deena? You sound a little funny," Roy asked.

"No . . . I mean, yes. Sure, I'm fine," Deena twisted the phone cord around her hand.

"If you say so. Could you tell Kathy I'm coming over?"

"Sure." Deena's thoughts were spinning.

"Thanks. See you." Roy hung up the phone and Deena just stood there for a moment, listening to the silence on the other end of the line.

57

Deena hung up the phone and started down the stairs. Her heartbeat quickened. She was torn between her curiosity to see what Kathy and Ken were doing, and dread of seeing them together.

As she entered the living room, she heard the sound of the ski video on the VCR. The coffee table and armchair were moved to one side, and Deena saw Kathy in the middle of the room, fully arrayed in ski equipment—boots, skis, poles, the works. *My* ski equipment! Deena realized. Ken was hovering nearby—nearer than he had to be, Deena thought. At first, neither of them took any notice of her. She quietly coughed.

"Oh, hi, Deena." Kathy glanced at Deena with a quick smile. "I borrowed your ski stuff for a while, O.K.? I needed it to take on treacherous Living Room Run."

Ken laughed at Kathy's joke, but it only made Deena angrier. "You could have asked me first, Kathy."

"Gee—I didn't think you would mind," Kathy said with a shrug.

"Oh, really? Well, I do. How would you like it if I took your roller skates? Or your oh-so-precious Walkman, and just used it without asking?"

"You hate to roller skate." Kathy seemed surprised at Deena's reaction. She awkwardly twisted around to face her.

"That's not the point!" Deena knew she was over-reacting, but she didn't know how to stop herself. She glanced over at Ken. He frowned and looked down at the worn-out rug, as if it was the most absolutely fascinating thing he'd ever seen. Now, on

58

top of everything, he thought she was a horrible shrew. She just wanted to die. "Never mind...it doesn't matter," she mumbled.

Feeling tears well up in her eyes, she quickly turned and ran out of the room.

Back up in the bedroom she slammed the door shut, then threw herself down on her bed. This had to be the worst day of her life!

Then she realized that she had never told Kathy Roy was coming over. He would be here any minute.

Oh, bother! Let Kathy handle it on her own. She seems to be doing all right for herself so far today, Deena thought. Miss Popularity certainly doesn't need *me* to manage her social life. Wiping the tears away from her eyes, Deena stared up at the ceiling. Besides, wild horses couldn't drag her back into the living room. She'd already made a complete fool of herself. Let fate take its course.

Deena didn't have long to wait to find out what fate had in store for her cousin. It wasn't long before she heard Roy's motorcycle roar up to the inn. Seconds later she heard the doorbell.

Ordinarily, Deena thought eavesdropping was simply unforgivable, but in this instance she just couldn't help herself. Some irresistible force drew her to the second-floor landing, where she could both hear and see what would happen next.

Still wearing Deena's ski boots, Kathy clopped out of the living room and opened the front door. She and Roy stood staring at each other for a second.

"Roy—hi . . . " Deena could hear the panic in her cousin's voice.

"Hi, Kath. What's doing?" Without waiting for Kathy to reply, Roy stepped inside. He unzipped his leather jacket. "Didn't Deena tell you I called? I had to stop by for the markers now because I have to watch Suzie later."

"Oh—I didn't know."

Roy shrugged. "Guess she forgot to tell you . . . What are you wearing those dumb ski boots for? Are they some new fashion or something?" Looking down at her feet, he started to laugh.

"I was just, uh, practicing some ski stuff. Polishing my skills."

"Your *skills*, huh?" Roy mimicked her in a gym-teacherish voice. "I thought you hated skiing. I thought you said it was the worst experience of your life—next to being forced to sit through a Barry Manilow concert on your grandmother's birthday."

"Well . . . " Kathy was just about quaking in her ski boots. But before she could come up with a feasible explanation for her sudden change of heart about skiing, Ken came out of the living room. One look at Roy's face, and she knew she might as well save her breath.

"Hi, Roy," Ken said pleasantly. Then Ken turned to Kathy and said, "The video is over. I'll rewind it, and we can watch that last part about S-turns again."

Here it comes, Deena thought. She wished she could see the expression on Kathy's face. But imagining was almost as good.

Roy glanced at Ken, then back at Kathy. "Looks like I

busted in on something. No wonder you didn't get my message."

"Roy, wait a second." Kathy tried to remain calm, even though her stomach was doing somersaults. "Let me go up and get the markers for you, O.K.?"

Roy barely listened to her. He was already walking toward the door. The look on his face was blank and unreadable. She tried to follow him, but in the ski boots she felt as if she were trying to chase after him with cement blocks on her feet.

"Don't bother." He opened the door. "Go back to your S-turns, Kathy," Roy said coolly. "Maybe a few U-turns, too. Just for good measure. I'm outta here . . . "

He was through the door before Kathy could say another word. She stamped her foot with frustration, then lost her balance, and fell down squarely on her bottom. "Ouch!"

"Hey—what happened? Let me help you up." Ken leaned over and offered her a hand.

"Oh, never mind. I'm O.K." Kathy waved him away. "I'm going to take these boots off while I'm down here." She sighed and began unfastening the buckles.

"Sure—I think we've done enough for one day." Ken was quiet for a moment as he watched Kathy pull off one boot and then the other. "It's getting late . . . I'd better go."

Kathy stood up. "O.K. Well, thanks for stopping by and all," she said awkwardly. "I really learned a lot from the tape."

"I'm glad. You can borrow it for a while if you want."

"Can I? Thanks. I'd like that."

"No problem. Maybe it will make you want to go skiing again sometime."

Kathy laughed. "Are you trying to brainwash me?"

"How do you think I get people to join the ski club?" Ken grabbed his down vest off the wooden coat rack near the door and put it on. "We lock them in a room and play the tape over and over. Works like a charm," he said as he opened the door. Deena winced.

Deena felt like crying. Some people hardly needed that much prodding, she thought, as she headed back to her room.

"See you in school tomorrow, Kathy," Ken said.

"See you." Kathy was honestly sorry to see Ken go. They had really been having fun. That is, until Roy dropped in. What if he didn't want to speak to her ever again? Wait until she cornered Deena! This was all her fault. How mean could a person be?

She closed the door and, without missing a beat, turned around and headed straight for the stairs. She felt like strangling Deena. Slowly. *Very* slowly.

By the time Kathy had climbed up the three flights of stairs, Deena was stretched out on her bed, paging through her biology textbook.

Kathy walked over to Deena's bed and stood there for a long moment, waiting for Deena to look up. Deena yawned lazily. "Ski lesson over so soon?"

Kathy looked like smoke was about to come pouring out of her ears. "Nice work, Deena. Very nice. I knew you were bent out of shape about me using your skis, but you could have told me Roy was coming over. That was a truly rotten thing to do. Now I'm really in a mess. I hope you're pleased with yourself."

"Poor Kathy! Can't keep track of her dates." Deena slammed her textbook closed and sat up. "Well, I'm not your personal secretary, in case you haven't figured it out. And besides, I *did* try to tell you Roy was coming, but you were too busy doing stem christies with Ken to even notice I was in the same room!"

"Not notice you! How could we *help* but notice you? You ran in there like a lunatic, and started screaming your head off about me using your dumb skis!" Deena cringed. She certainly didn't need to be reminded of how foolish she must have looked. "I had to explain to Ken that you only act like that when the moon is full."

"Very funny!" Deena sprang off her bed and paced across the room. "I'm sure you didn't tell him that you act like a lunatic *all* the time."

"At least I don't act like a sneaky, slimy snake!" Kathy shot back. "I know you don't like Roy and will do anything to keep his *uncouth* presence from polluting the atmosphere around here. But that was just plain low-down and mean. How can you stand yourself?"

"Me! How can *I* stand *myself*!?" Deena echoed incredulously. You steal away the guy I really like, and you have the nerve to ask me that question? she wanted to yell back at her. But remembering her promise to herself, she bit down on her lip. "I can't believe this conversation! The question is, how can *you* stand *yourself*? Or stand wallowing in that utter pigpen on your side of this room!

63

Or stand to hang around with any of your moronic friends!"

"And your side of the room is so great! That *gorgeous* bedspread makes your bed look like a float from the Easter Parade. It has so many ruffles on it, I could puke! And your friends are all nerds—like you—who don't know how to have any fun."

"Well, my friends *don't* shave their heads and paint themselves blue, if that's what you mean. But most people stopped calling that 'fun' right about the time Prehistoric Man learned how to walk upright!"

"Oh, you are so-o-o smart, Deena! I am so-o-o impressed."

It was Kathy's night to start dinner, and she didn't have any more time to stand there arguing with her cousin. "I'm going down to put the casserole in the oven. It's your favorite, macaroni and cheese...All *rats* love cheese, don't they?" she asked sweetly as she slipped out the door.

Deena was so angry at Kathy she could have thrown something at her. But she was also miserable with herself. She lay down and had herself a good cry.

* * *

Deena and Kathy somehow managed to get through dinner an hour later without blowing up at each other again. Their ceasefire was maintained only because they each refused to acknowledge the other's presence. When Kathy wanted the salad dressing passed to her from Deena's end of the table, the message was relayed through her brother, Johnny. "Salad dressing. Here's the long pass," Johnny said in his sportscaster voice. "First down!"

The same thing happened when Deena asked for the bread, which was sitting just inches from Kathy's nose. And of course, their hostility made everyone else tense.

Their mothers exchanged silent glances, but neither commented on the state of war between their daughters until dessert.

"I don't know what's going on with you two tonight," Deena's mother said finally. "But you had better talk it over privately and start treating each other in a civil manner."

"Where is this coming from, girls?" Kathy's mother added. Deena rolled her eyes to the ceiling. She hated it when her aunt started talking California-cosmic. "You two are giving off negative energy all over the place. Work on it. It's not fair to the rest of us."

"O.K., Mom," Kathy said, getting up from the table. "I'm going to do my homework . . . and recharge my battery. See you later."

In order to avoid Deena until bedtime, Kathy took her school books down to the living room. Johnny was watching a TV show that had a car crash about every ten seconds, but the noise didn't bother Kathy at all. In fact, she thought it helped keep her awake while she tried to read her impossibly boring Dickens novel.

At about nine o'clock she decided to call Roy. She knew he was home alone watching his little sister, so he didn't have any way to duck her call. Or so she thought.

The phone rang three times, then she heard Roy's father's voice on an answering machine. She hung up without leaving a message.

Kathy was sitting in front of the phone, trying to decide whether or not to call back and leave Roy a message on the tape, when the phone rang. She was positive he'd heard the click on the message tape and figured out it was her.

"Hello?" she said eagerly.

"Hi, Kathy," Ken's voice greeted her. "I hope I'm not calling too late."

"Oh, hi, Ken . . . No, not at all. I was just finishing my homework. I have an English test tomorrow, on *A Tale of Two Cities* by Charles Dickens. I can't *believe* this guy. I mean, the way he writes, I think his motto was 'Why say it with one word when you can use ten?' I told Mrs. Godfrey that I think *A Tale of One City* would have been *plenty*."

Ken laughed. "I'll try not to keep you on the phone too long, then. When I was over this afternoon, I forgot to ask you something. A friend of mine is having a party this Saturday night and . . . well, I was wondering if you wanted to maybe go to it with me?" Ken asked in a rush. "I mean, if you're not busy or anything."

Kathy got the feeling Ken was hinting about Roy. Roy hadn't asked her out for Saturday night, and Kathy was almost positive that she wouldn't be seeing him at all this weekend. Unless we run into each other by accident, she thought. As in Roy *accidently* running me over with his motorcycle.

"Uh—no, I don't have any plans. The party sounds like fun. I'd love to go with you."

"Great," Ken said. "Well, good luck on your test tomorrow. I'll look for you in the cafeteria."

They said good night, and Kathy hung up. Then she dialed Roy's number again and left a brief message. She had the feeling he wouldn't call her back, and she really felt bad. But then she thought about Ken. He was a really nice guy once you got past the boy-scout part.

"So you think you're so tough, Roy Harris," Kathy mumbled to herself as she flipped open her book again. "Don't pick up your stupid phone. See what I care. As this guy Dickens might say, 'It is a far, far dumber thing than you've ever done before.'"

Chapter 6

Kathy was one of the last people in class to finish her English exam. She knew she didn't ace it by a long shot, but she was sure that she had at least passed. Not bad, considering that last night she had desperately tried to speed-read most of the four-hundred-page novel in one sitting. About halfway through, Kathy suddenly realized that she had seen an old movie version of the Dickens classic on TV a few weeks ago, when she had been home sick with a cold. Once again Hollywood had saved her neck in Mrs. Godfrey's class, for which Kathy was eternally grateful.

As usual, the hallway was a zoo between classes, with books, clothes, and even bodies hurling in all directions. Kathy took her lunch out of her locker and tossed some books in. Her locker was about as orderly as the inside of a wastepaper basket, and it was always a challenge to jam the door shut again.

In the cafeteria she looked around for Ellecia, Zee, and Roy. Then she remembered that Zee was absent today, Ellecia had to make up a Spanish test this period, and, of course, Roy was purposely trying to avoid her as he had all morning.

Feeling glum, Kathy sat down at an empty table and took out her sandwich. She hated eating lunch alone. Once in a while when she was absolutely desperate, she sat with Deena and her friends. She could see them a few tables away. But she still wasn't speaking to Deena, and Kathy certainly wasn't going to make the first move to make up. Not this time, she told herself. Deena could just stew in her own juice. Or her own "bad vibes," as her mother would say.

"Hey, Kathy." Kathy's thoughts were interrupted by Ken's cheerful greeting. "Why are you sitting here all alone? Are you waiting for somebody?"

"Uh—no. None of my friends seem to be around today." Kathy gulped down a bite of her sandwich. Ken was wearing a white turtleneck under a turquoise sweater that made his eyes look even bluer than usual. He sure looked cute today, she thought.

"Why don't you come over and sit with me—me and my friends, I mean. Here, I'll help you with your stuff."

Ken balanced her container of chocolate milk on her books, and Kathy took her sandwich and purse. She was a little nervous about eating lunch at Ken's table. All the super-popular people in school sat there. But what the heck. As Ken said, "No guts, no glory."

A few minutes later Deena's friend Pat Rogus nudged Deena's arm. "Hey—look who your cousin Kathy is eating lunch with today. She's sitting at *the* table."

Deena glanced up and saw Kathy a few tables away, sitting next to Ken, among all his friends. She felt like somebody had just punched her in the stomach. But she tried her best to act unimpressed. "So she is—maybe she's collecting for a needy rock group. Maybe one of her idols needs a brain transplant."

Deena's friends started laughing. Everyone but Pat, who was Deena's closest friend and who was the one person Deena had told of her crush on Ken. Pat was also one of the smartest people in Deena's grade, so there wasn't much that got past her.

After lunch, when the two girls were alone walking to class, Pat said, "I thought you really liked Ken Buckly. Doesn't it bother you that Kathy was hanging out with him?"

Deena just shrugged. "I think he's a nice guy. But I only like him as a friend." She stopped at her locker and put some books away. Her textbooks were arranged in size order on the top shelf, and she hated to mix them up. "I thought I really liked him before . . . before I got to know him better. But I don't really think he's my type."

Pat gave Deena a quizzical look, but didn't ask her any more questions. Deena was relieved. It was hard to pre-

70

tend she didn't like Ken and didn't care if he liked Kathy. But Deena hoped that if she pretended long enough, it would really be true.

During the next few days, Deena's acting abilities were really put to the test. Ken came over to see Kathy almost every afternoon or evening. Deena tried to avoid seeing him when he was at the inn by either busying herself with some project in another part of the house or going out herself.

Kathy might accuse her of being a low-down sneak, but Deena knew she would never knowingly try to steal him away from Kathy by making excuses to hang around with them or flirting with him when she wasn't there.

Not that she fooled herself into thinking for one instant that using those tactics would get any results. Ken seemed totally enthralled with Kathy. Everything that Deena thought would drive him crazy about her cousin—because it drove *her* crazy—seemed to fascinate him. Her funky clothes, her taste in music, her disinterest in school—or anything even remotely intellectual—and her generally weird outlook on the universe seemed to totally charm Ken. He acted as if she were the most worldy wise person he'd ever met, and was awed by the fact that she had lived in California—as if there weren't about two zillion other people who could make the same claim. Sometimes, overhearing their conversations, Deena thought she was going to gag.

However, there was one advantage Deena found to the whole sorry mess. Now that she knew she didn't have a chance with Ken, she was able to relax and be herself around him. If she happened to be in the living room watching TV while Ken was waiting for Kathy to come downstairs, they always seemed to find plenty to talk about.

On Thursday Ken stopped over unexpectedly after school. Kathy wasn't home yet, and Deena was playing Clue with Johnny. Ken decided to stick around and try to figure out the mystery, too.

"I feel it's only fair to warn you guys," Ken said as he sat down, "my brothers call me Sherlock Holmes. I always figure out who done it."

Deena shuffled out the cards without saying a word.

"I bet you're not better than Deena," Johnny piped in. "She's the best."

"Oh, really . . ." Ken glanced over at Deena. "All right, Miss Peacock," Ken said, using the character name of the game marker Deena had picked. "Let's play for the Cranford Clue Championship Title. O.K.?"

"You're on, Colonel Mustard," Deena said brightly. She was an absolute whiz at this game.

By the time Kathy came home, Deena had won three games out of three.

"I can't believe it. I've been shut out!" Ken wailed, amazed that she'd gotten the solution to the last round so quickly.

"Hi, guys," Kathy said, walking into the living room. "What's going on?"

"Your cousin is a genius," Ken announced to Kathy as

he got up off the floor. "Come on, Deena. How did you know it was Professor Plum?"

"Elementary, my dear Buckly," Deena quipped.

Kathy shook her head. "I think I missed something. But never mind. I never really liked that game anyway."

Deena left the living room and went upstairs. It had been fun to spend some time with Ken, even if they had only played a silly board game. Maybe they could be friends after all, she thought.

* * *

On Saturday night Kathy began to get ready for the party at Ken's friend's house. The major question of the evening was what to wear. Kathy tried on and pulled off every piece of clothing she owned. Nothing looked right, and her side of the room, which was always messy, now looked as if it had been hit by a tidal wave.

"Ugh! Why did I ever buy this shirt! It makes me look like a bag lady!"

Without looking up from her magazine, Deena commented, "Really? I thought the bag lady look was the basic goal of your wardrobe."

She was going out in a little while also, to the movies with Pat and some other friends. She was dressed in what Kathy called the Ivory Girl look—cream-colored corduroy pants, tan Topsiders, and a yellow Shetland wool sweater that had an intricate snowflake design around the yoke. Her hair was pulled back with a yellow ribbon.

Kathy glanced at her cousin's reflection in the mirror, realizing that Deena had tons of clothes that would be just perfect for this party. Then she got annoyed at herself for getting so bent out of shape over making a good impression on Ken's friends. Get hold of yourself! Would you actually be seen in public dressed like Deena?

No way! She would dress like she always did—as if she were going out with Ellecia and Roy and her usual gang. She hadn't seen much of them in the past week, and Roy still wouldn't talk to her at school, or answer her calls. But Kathy decided to worry about that later.

Tonight she was going to put on her new black leather miniskirt and really have a good time. Ken always liked the way she dressed. Well, at least he always said the things she wore were "very interesting." His friends would think so, too, Kathy told herself.

While putting on her eye make-up in the bathroom, Kathy suddenly got a daring idea. Last week Zee had brought over a can of something called Hair Graffitti—a type of temporary hair color that came in outrageous colors. You just sprayed it in and presto—instant neon streaks. She'd had a blast with Zee and Ellecia fooling around with the stuff. Impulsively Kathy grabbed the can of spray and gave herself a subtle electric blue streak. Just the right touch for my outfit, she thought as she admired the results.

Ken and Kathy were the last to arrive at the party. The music was already blaring—some soft-rock, bubble-gum tune that made Kathy's skin crawl. One of Deena's favorite groups, of course. Ken's friends seemed to be really enjoying it. People were dancing and laughing, or just hanging out.

When she and Ken walked in, however, Kathy got the eerie feeling that for a moment everyone had stopped to stare at her. As she had guessed, *everyone* there, guys and girls, were dressed like Deena, right down to their preppie deck shoes.

There was not a single scrap of black leather in the room besides her own miniskirt and ankle-high black boots. Unless you counted the dog collar on the family's Labrador retriever, which Ellecia would have worn as a necklace. Kathy knew she was in trouble when she realized that so far, she had more in common with Rover than anyone else in the room.

With the miniskirt, she was wearing a purple shirt with a squiggle black design and her banana earrings. She also had on a black silk basketball jacket that said BOWL-O-RAMA on the back in red letters. It might have been her imagination, or her own nervousness, but Kathy thought she heard Ken stop and take a deep breath before leading them into the party.

Then, smiling as usual, he introduced her to some of his friends whom she hadn't already met in the cafeteria this week.

As the party continued, Kathy tried her best not to feel like a visitor from another planet. But everyone was talking about things she had absolutely no interest in—the standings of local high school basketball teams, horseback riding, or the Holly Ball, which was a big dance that the Cranford Women's Club sponsored annually around the holidays. Deena and her friends were dying to go to it, Kathy knew. She cracked up laughing every time she saw them mooning over pictures of prom gowns in magazines.

It wasn't that people didn't talk to her. But when Ken wasn't standing right next to her, Kathy felt a chilly blast from some of his friends—particularly a group of girls who had been whispering and laughing when she came in.

"Aren't you Deena Scott's cousin?" one girl named Janet said to her. "You live in that big old hotel on Haymarket Road, right?"

"That place always gives me the creeps when I drive by," another girl said. "It looks haunted."

Kathy forced herself to laugh. "It did look pretty bad when we moved in this summer. But it's really shaping up—we've been painting and fixing up the rooms really nice. We're going to be open for business next week."

"Sounds great," Janet said with a simpering smile. "Were you painting today, too, Kathy?"

"Uh—no," Kathy said, a bit puzzled by the question.

"Oh, I was just wondering if that's how you got that blue streak in your hair," Janet added innocently. She sipped her soda as the other girls laughed.

"Oh, I put it there on purpose," Kathy shot back. She forced herself to sound cool, even though inside she was fuming.

"Really? Why?" another girl asked her between giggles.

Kathy shrugged. "It's a new style. You know, as in the

twentieth century? Well, for people in New York and San Francisco. Hip places, I mean. But I guess news travels slowly out here to the back woods." Kathy forced a laugh and took a sip of her diet soda.

The other girls just stared at her. They were speechless. She smiled at them and looked down at her empty cup. "Think I'll get some more soda. See you later."

Feeling as if smoke were pouring out of her ears, she worked her way through the group to the other side of the room. Ken was hanging out there with his ski club buddies. She could hear the girls snickering behind her back and once again felt as if everyone was watching her.

She stuck pretty close to Ken for the rest of the night. They danced for a while, and Kathy knew that even the girls who had made fun of her were impressed by her great moves. The music, of course, was a major handicap.

"Having a good time, Kathy?" Ken asked when they took a break from dancing.

"Oh, sure. Great party," she told him.

"I'm glad. I know my friends are pretty different from yours," he said quietly. "But I can tell they really think you're something special."

Kathy forced a smile. She just didn't have the heart to tell Ken that his friends thought she was about as "special" as the fat lady at the circus—just another sideshow freak. And they would probably all agree that the fat lady dressed better.

"I'm getting hungry. Let's get something to eat," Kathy said, trying to change the subject.

Finally the evening was over, and Ken drove her back to the inn. Kathy was exhausted. This had been one of the longest dates of her life. She'd had a better time at the dentist!

Ken pulled up at the front of the inn and walked Kathy to the front door. "Well, good night, Kath," he said. "I had a real good time tonight. Thanks for coming with me."

"Thanks for inviting me," Kathy said. She did like Ken. It wasn't his fault his friends were such a bunch of toads.

"Listen, if you're not doing anything tomorrow afternoon, some of my friends are getting together at my house to watch the football game on TV. Want to come?"

Watch football? With the same group that she had just narrowly escaped? The very thought made Kathy feel as if she was going to break out in a rash. "Gee—I don't think I can make it, Ken. I have to help out around here tomorrow. We still have a lot to do before opening day."

"Oh, sure. I understand," Ken said. "Maybe some other time." He leaned over and gave Kathy a soft, sweet kiss. Then he playfully pulled on one of her earrings. "These earrings are...really...umm...interesting, Kath," he said.

"Thanks." Kathy decided to take the comment as a compliment—the only one she had received all night. "See you." She opened the door and went inside.

"Good night," Ken said. With a brief wave, he bounded down the porch steps and got back into his car.

When Kathy got inside, she heard the TV and her mother and aunt talking in the living room. She walked in and sat down in the old rocker.

"How was the party?" her mother asked. "Did you have a good time?"

"It was O.K.," Kathy said with a shrug.

"Just O.K.?" her aunt asked sympathetically.

"I danced a lot," Kathy said, rocking back and forth. "I guess I'll go up to bed now." She kissed her mother and aunt good night.

"Take off those dancing shoes and rest up, kiddo," her mother said. "You and Deena have some major decorating jobs to tackle tomorrow."

"I'll be up early," Kathy promised.

Up in her room she quickly got undressed in the dark. Deena was already asleep, and she didn't want to wake her. That party had been a real downer, Kathy thought as she slipped under the covers. And when Ken kissed her good night . . . well, she just didn't feel the same as when Roy kissed her.

Kathy sighed out loud thinking about Roy. Why did he have to act like such a big baby? Boys were really jerks sometimes. On Monday it would be an entire week since he'd last spoken to her. She tried to get Ellecia to find out how he felt. But her friend hadn't been able to worm much out of him. As a matter of fact, even Ellecia hadn't been acting that friendly toward her the past few days. Once or twice Ellecia had made a snide comment about Kathy's new connection to Ken and his friends, but Kathy had pretended not to notice. She really thought Ellecia was jealous, and besides, she was a free citizen, for goodness' sake. Just because she was friends with Ellecia, Zee, and Roy, it didn't mean she couldn't hang out with Ken when she felt like it.

Kathy sighed again and punched up her pillow. She flopped over to her side, but couldn't get comfortable. In the shadowy light she could see the outline of Deena's sleeping form. Her cousin never had problems like this. Her friends were always so polite to each other. It was weird.

Kathy wondered if she should ask Deena's advice. Maybe she would know how to handle Roy and Ellecia, and Ken's friends, too. Deena was really on Ken's wavelength. Kathy had noticed that from the few times she'd overheard them talking about school, or skiing, or other things that interested them both.

Bag that idea, Kathy thought as she punched up her pillow again. Deena would go into her know-it-all "Dear Abby" act, and she would never let Kathy forget that she'd come to her for advice. No, she wouldn't ask Deena for advice about this. She'd have to work it out on her own.

Chapter 7

The officers of the ski club had called a special meeting for sixth period on Wednesday. The club's next trip was supposed to take place on the Saturday after Thanksgiving. But so far hardly any of the plans were in order.

It was Deena's lunch period, so she bought a container of juice and then went to the empty classroom where the meeting was being held. No one was there yet, except for Ken. She was embarrassed to be the first one to arrive, but he seemed happy to see her.

"Finally—signs of life! For a minute there, I was afraid that I was going to have this meeting all by myself."

"Hi, Ken." Deena took a seat near him, and began taking out her lunch. Since Ken had been hanging around the inn so much lately to see Kathy, Deena didn't feel shy around him anymore. Well, maybe just a twinge here and there, when she let herself remember how much she still liked him. Being all alone with him right now was making her remember.

"I'm sure other people will be here soon," she said lightly. "They probably just stopped to get something to eat."

"I stopped in the cafeteria to get a burger, but the line was in super-gridlock. I knew I'd be stuck in there all afternoon. All I could grab was some milk and potato chips from the vending machine."

Deena had already unwrapped her sandwich and was about to take a bite. "Would you like some of my sandwich?" she asked, hesitantly. "It's peanut butter and shredded carrot, on whole wheat. With raisins." The combination was one of Deena's favorites—but saying it out loud to Ken, it sure sounded silly. He was probably going to think she had some kind of weird food fetish.

"Peanut butter and carrot?" he echoed, as if he thought he hadn't heard her right.

"I know it sounds strange . . . but it's really good. And very nutritious," Deena said, feeling even more foolish.

"I *know*—I eat it all the time," Ken burst out laughing. "I just didn't think anyone else in the entire world liked peanut butter and carrot . . . "

"With raisins," she cut in. She felt mildly elated that Ken—of all people—was the only person she'd ever met who actually liked her favorite sandwich.

"I never tried it with raisins."

"Here," Deena handed him a half. "It's the best."

"Gee—thanks. This looks great." Ken took a big bite. "Hey—this is even better with raisins," he mumbled around a mouthful of sandwich.

After gobbling down Deena's sandwich, they shared Ken's potato chips. A few more people straggled in and the meeting finally got under way.

The first order of business was to appoint someone to collect the money for the next ski trip. Ken was making the arrangements for the buses, rental equipment, and lessons, so it didn't seem fair for him to do that job too.

When no one volunteered, Deena decided to offer. "I'll do it, Ken," she said.

"Are you sure you'll have the time? I know you and Kathy are busy right now, getting the inn ready for opening day."

Deena winced at the mention of her cousin's name. It was as if a cool wind had blown through the room, robbing her of the warm feeling she'd had when she and Ken were sharing her sandwich.

"I can do it," Deena said, forcing herself not to think about Kathy and Ken. "I'll get my mom to help me set up the list on our home computer. It will only take a few minutes."

Ken seemed impressed. "That sounds great. We'll really be able to keep track of things this time. I didn't know you had a computer at home."

"Oh, you didn't?" It wasn't exactly something Kathy would mention, mainly because she didn't know how to use the computer and didn't have the patience to learn. "Next time you come over, I'll show it to you," she said.

When the meeting was over Deena went to the cafeteria to look for her friends. She was surprised to see Kathy sitting with Ellecia again, and not at her new table, with Ken's friends. Deena noticed Roy wasn't sitting with the two girls, however. She figured he must still be angry at her cousin. Deena felt a niggling twinge of guilt about that. Even though she knew it wasn't totally her fault. Oh, what's the sense of worrying about that now? Kathy probably didn't even care if she saw Roy anymore, now that she was hanging out with Ken and his friends. Besides, Deena thought, what can I do about smoothing things over between Kathy and Roy? Roy and I *barely* speak the same language.

Deena found her friend Pat, who was sitting by herself, catching up on some homework. Pat was quite willing to leave her assignment unfinished, however, once Deena sat down. Deena pushed Kathy out of her mind as she began to chat with her friend.

On the other side of the cafeteria, Kathy was not exactly having a pleasant chat with her friend Ellecia. Far from it, in fact. When Kathy had sat down, Ellecia had not seemed particularly thrilled to see her.

Kathy acted as if she didn't notice, but she knew Ellecia was wondering why she wasn't sitting with Ken's friends again today. The truth was, when Ken wasn't there, Kathy felt odd sitting at that table. Especially after the way some of his friends had acted toward her last Saturday night. She'd been eager to sit at her old table again, but had never expected her friends to act so cool to her here as well.

"So, how was that party last Saturday night?" Ellecia finally asked her.

"O.K., I guess—well, really, it was kind of weird. I was the only one in the room who was wearing black leather—except for the dog," Kathy said, making Ellecia laugh. "And the music made me gag. I should have brought my Walkman."

"That reminds me, did you hear about the Pinheads concert? They're going to play at the arena in Barnesville. One night only. A bunch of us are getting tickets. Want to go?"

"The Pinheads? Really?" Next to Nuclear Waste, they were her favorite group. Kathy couldn't believe that she hadn't heard that they were coming into the area. She was really getting out of touch these days. "I'd love to go! When is it?"

"Next weekend, the Saturday after Thanksgiving."

"Gee—I don't know if that's going to work out for me." What rotten luck! Why did it have to be the Saturday after Thanksgiving?

Ellecia could not imagine what could be more important to Kathy than a chance to see the Pinheads, live in concert. "What's the matter? Do you have to stick around and help at the inn? I thought the Grand Opening bash was on Thanksgiving Day?"

"It is. I mean, I can go out Saturday night, that's no problem," Kathy said hesitantly, not knowing whether she should confide the real reason to Ellecia. "It's just that I made plans with Ken to go skiing that day, and I don't know if I'll be back in time to go to the concert, too."

"Oh, sure. I get the concept," Ellecia said huffily.

Kathy saw the expression on her friend's face and got a knot in her stomach. Ellecia was getting cool and distant again, the way she had been when Kathy had first sat down. Only now it was ten times worse.

"Too bad. You're really going to miss the rock event of the year . . . to go *skiing* with the King of the Prepheads." Ellecia said the word *skiing* as if Kathy had said she preferred to stay home and put mothballs in her closet, or get her stamp collection in order, or some other unbelievably nerdy activity.

"Come on, Ellecia," Kathy pleaded. "Give me a break." All she needed now was to get into a fight with Ellecia, *too*.

"No—you come on, Kathy. What's the take on you anyway, lately?"

"What do you mean?" Kathy asked, although she knew very well what Ellecia meant.

"I mean, it's like ever since the human Ken doll came on the scene, you've been acting like Barbie. It's really gross."

"I have not. I haven't been acting any different at all."

"Oh, really? Guess *again*, Kathy." Ellecia's tone made Kathy shiver with apprehension. "I'm glad you're so-o-o *popular* now. Goody, goody for you. Maybe you should try out for the cheerleading squad."

Cheerleading! Kathy took a deep breath. Low blow!

And from her best friend! All she had done was sit at a different lunch table for a few days. Did she really deserve this?

"Listen, I didn't say I absolutely wasn't going to the concert. It's just that I have these other plans. Maybe I can switch things around."

"Suit yourself," Ellecia said. "Roy is picking up tickets at the mall for everyone this afternoon. If you want to go, you'd better tell him before school is over."

"O.K., I will," Kathy replied, sounding a lot more definite about it than she felt.

She was really nervous about talking to Roy. He had been avoiding her for over a week. At least now she had an excuse to speak to him. Maybe it wouldn't be so bad.

When her last class of the day ended, Kathy went straight to Roy's locker. He was already there, shrugging into his leather jacket. She took a deep breath and walked up to him.

"Hi, Roy. Umm—are you in a hurry?"

Roy looked up at her. He looked surprised for a second—and almost happy—Kathy thought. But that look flickered in his dark eyes for just an instant. Maybe she imagined it.

"Yeah—kind of. What do you want?" It was the same tone he used to talk to his pesty little sister, Kathy noticed. With a quick, familiar motion, he brushed the thick dark hair back off his forehead with his hand. Kathy realized that she had really missed him these past few days.

"Ellecia told me about that Pinheads concert, and I was thinking of going."

"Oh—you want me to get you a ticket, you mean?" Roy asked, sounding slightly more friendly. Not much, but slightly.

"Well, I really want to go . . . but I might not be able to make it, so I was wondering how much the ticket was, in case I got stuck with it . . . "

"Why would you get stuck with the ticket?" Roy's gaze narrowed, and he crossed his arms over his chest.

"I—uh, have other plans for the day, and I might not be home in time to go to the concert, too," Kathy said, nervously glancing down the hallway for a second. She was not going to make the same mistake with Roy that she had made with Ellecia—confessing what those other plans were.

Unfortunately, Kathy didn't have to go into detail with Roy. He guessed easily what was going on. "You mean other plans with your *other* friends, right?"

The longer Roy looked at her with that hard stare and his arms folded across his chest, the more nervous Kathy got. She felt like just saying "Forget it" and running down the hall in the opposite direction. Why had she ever tried to talk to him in the first place?

"I just have plans, that's all."

Roy looked down and kicked a scrap of paper with the toe of his boot. "Yeah, well . . . you can't be in two places at once, you know what I mean, Kathy? I mean, it's physically impossible."

"I know *that*," Kathy said, not really understanding why he sounded so serious about something so obvious.

When Roy got into one of his philosophical moods, trying to keep up could really overload a person's circuits.

"No—" Roy shook his head, his lips pursed in a frown—"I don't think you're really getting it. I mean, your head, Kathy. Where is it at? It can't be in two places at once. You can't ride around in Ken Buckly's BMW Saturday morning—and on the back of my bike Saturday night."

Kathy felt stunned, as if Roy had just dashed her with a bucket of cold water. Roy didn't say much, but he was a lot more observant and sensitive than most people ever imagined. Kathy had always admired his way of seeing right through people who were phoney. But not right now, when he was using his x-ray vision on her.

"Roy—I think you're making a big deal out of nothing," Kathy tried to sound calm, even though she felt as if she was about to cry.

"O.K., Kathy. Whatever you say." Roy shrugged. "But I don't even think you like hanging out with those jocks. You're just doing it for status or something. Because all of a sudden Ken Buckly drives you home from school a few times, and everyone around here knows your name. And I know you were at a party with him and his friends on Saturday night, too."

"How did you know that?"

"I just know, O.K.?" Roy turned around and slammed his locker closed, then snapped the lock closed and twirled it. "So if you're having such a good time with Ken and his friends, why do you want to see the Pinheads with us? Why don't you get some of your new friends to go?"

Kathy knew she had about as much chance of getting Ken's friends to go to that concert as she had persuading them to shave off all their hair and tattoo the rock group's rally cry, "Pinheads Unite and Rock All Night," across their foreheads. Of course, she'd never admit that to Roy.

"Maybe I will," she shot back angrily. "So you can just forget I ever asked you about that stupid ticket, O.K.?"

Kathy spun around and started pushing her way through the crowded corridor. She couldn't get away from Roy Harris fast enough.

He was mean. He was horrible. How could she have ever thought for one minute that she liked him? And even missed him besides? If she ever spoke a single word to him again, it would be too soon. And she certainly didn't want him to see that she was crying.

Chapter 8

Kathy could not imagine a worse way of spending a Friday night than being stuck at home, painting the second-floor hallway with Deena. But if she didn't do something about it quick, that's exactly what was going to happen.

The girls had started the job right after school. At first it looked as if it would only take them a few hours to do it. But it was one of those days when the more they worked, the more wall space there seemed left to paint. As if the hallway were mysteriously growing every time they turned around, like something out of *Alice in Wonderland*.

"I'm pooped," Deena announced at five o'clock. She tossed her roller in the paint pan and wiped her hands off with a rag. "Let's take a break, Kathy. Want another diet soda?"

"A break?" Kathy didn't stop painting for a second. "We can't take a break—I thought we were going to try and finish this by supper?"

"No way—we still have all the trim and the doors. And there's that patch on the ceiling you missed before..."

"I didn't forget. Listen, you take a break if you want. I'm going to keep working." Kathy dipped her roller in the paint pan and slapped it on the wall, painting away at a feverish pace.

Deena watched her for a few moments. What had gotten into Kathy? she wondered. She'd never seen her cousin attack a job around the house with such zeal. It was strange. Maybe the paint fumes had gone to her brain.

"Kathy—slow down. This isn't a race. You're splashing paint all over the place."

"No, I'm not. Go have your soda. By the time you get back, this whole wall will be finished. I promise."

Deena was unbelievably slow when she painted. She acted as if she were working on a masterpiece that was going to hang in a museum. By the time she did two inches of molding, Kathy had the whole ceiling painted—except that spot she missed in her hurry.

Deena stood behind Kathy as she was wildly swinging the paint roller in haphazard directions. "Kathy, you're supposed to push the roller in one direction, up and down. Otherwise, it comes out all wrong."

"Deena—I know how to paint, for goodness—" As

Deena reached over for the roller to show Kathy what she meant, Kathy swung around without realizing that her cousin was standing right behind her. And Kathy's reply was cut short by a loud splat as the sopping wet roller in her hand landed directly in the middle of Deena's chest. "Oh ... darn ... Sorry."

"Yuck!" Deena shrieked and jumped back as if Kathy were armed and dangerous. "What a mess! Just look at me!"

Kathy tossed the roller into the paint pan and stood with her hands on her hips. Her cousin was such a fuss-budget. She could paint for hours without getting one single spot on herself. It made Kathy crazy. Looks like she made up for it all in one shot today, though, Kathy thought, trying not to laugh.

"Oh, calm down, will you?" Kathy said. "I said I was sorry. It was an accident. Most normal people get a few spots on their clothes when they paint, Deena."

"A few spots? You just gave me a bath in it." Deena wriggled uncomfortably under her paint-soaked sweat shirt. "Sometimes you are just so careless, Kathy. And you did such a sloppy job on that part of the wall, we're going to have to paint it over after dinner anyway. Haste makes waste," Deena added primly as she wiped off her face. The little droplets of paint were already dry, and her attempt to wipe them off only smeared them into powder blue streaks.

"What is all the racket about up here?" Kathy's mother appeared at the top of the stairway. The two girls turned toward her, both talking at once.

"Kathy hit me with a paint roller! She's making a mess of everything!"

"Deena thinks she's an art critic or something! I paint two inches, and I have to hear her *review* for an hour! 'It's not straight. It's too thick. It's too thin,'" Kathy whined, mimicking her cousin to perfection.

"Girls—slow down. I don't understand a word of this." Nancy looked at each of them, her gaze coming to rest on Deena's messy sweat shirt.

"Stop that! I do not sound like that," Deena replied to Kathy. "If it weren't for me, you'd take the bucket of paint and just glob it on the wall—as if you were loading up ketchup on a pile of fries. Which is *truly* a vision of grossness to see."

"Oh, yeah? Well, I bet when you were a little kid you cried every time your crayon slipped and you went outside the lines in your coloring book. You are such a neatness freak!"

"O.K.—I've heard *enough*," Nancy shouted in her referee voice. "I think you girls need a break," she said in a calmer voice. "You've been working hard all afternoon. I want you to both clean up now and take a rest. You can finish up here after supper."

"I was supposed to go out after supper," Kathy said, folding her arms over her chest. "To the movies, with Ken and some of his friends."

"Oh, O.K. Well, don't worry about it, Kathy. You can go to the movies. I'll finish here with Deena later," her mother told her.

Deena, who had calmed down somewhat a few moments ago, felt her temper rising all over again. *Ken! Ken! Ken!* That's all Kathy talked about lately. Every other word out of her mouth was about either Ken or Ken's friends. Deena had tried her best to ignore it but she was getting sick and tired of this.

And now her aunt was going to let Kathy off the hook tonight to go out and have fun with *Ken* while Deena was stuck here working. It just wasn't fair! Deena knew that if the situation were reversed, her mother wouldn't care if she had a date with Prince Charles.

"That's not fair! If Kathy's not painting tonight, I'm not, either," Deena blurted out.

Her own mother would have probably been angry if Deena had answered back that way. But Aunt Nancy was different about things like that. She believed that everyone had the right to express their feelings—even teenagers.

She gave Deena a sympathetic look. "You're right. That isn't very fair, is it?" she said, patting Deena's arm. "I was thinking of taking a ride into town to get a movie for the VCR tonight. Why don't you change and come with me, Deena? And both you girls can finish this up tomorrow morning."

"O.K.," Deena said quietly, nodding at her aunt. She didn't know why, but all of a sudden, she felt like crying.

"Good—I'll be downstairs in the kitchen."

After Nancy went downstairs, Kathy and Deena began to clean up the paint and rollers and other equipment.

"Hey, Deena—I'm sorry I hit you with the roller," Kathy said as she banged the lid on a can of paint. "I didn't mean it, honest."

Deena nodded. "I know. I'm sorry I made fun of the way you eat fries."

"That's O.K. Roy says the same thing. I mean, he used to . . . " Kathy shrugged and took a deep breath. "Listen, I'll wash out your sweat shirt for you later."

"Don't bother. It's just a raggy old thing I wear for working around the house. It'll be all right once it dries."

As Deena headed for the bathroom to change, it was Kathy's turn to think her cousin had gotten lightheaded from the paint fumes.

After Kathy had gone out, Deena watched the movie *Top Gun* with her mother, Aunt Nancy, and Johnny. They all enjoyed it. But Tom Cruise just kept reminding Deena of Ken.

It wasn't Kathy's fault that she was going out with Ken, Deena decided. Looking back, Deena could see now that she actually encouraged the situation that first day, by not warning Kathy that Roy was stopping by. Deena got the feeling Kathy still really liked Roy better than Ken. In fact, she had overheard Kathy on the phone, talking to Ellecia about Roy. It sounded like Kathy and Roy had had another fight about something after school yesterday, and now things were worse than ever between them. Kathy had sounded really upset over it. If she were really happy with Ken, Deena reasoned, she wouldn't give a hoot about Roy.

But what could she do about smoothing things over

between Kathy and Roy? Deena just couldn't see a way to make up for the problem she'd caused.

With a sigh, Deena decided that she would just try to be nicer to Kathy and not allow her own feelings for Ken to get in the way. It made everyone in the family miserable when she and Kathy argued, and with the Grand Opening coming up, they had enough to worry about, Deena thought.

Meanwhile, Kathy sat beside Ken in the movie theater and stared blankly at the flickering images. She couldn't understand why, but ever since her last fight with Roy, she had felt really self-conscious around Ken. It was as if she was watching herself, trying to figure out if what Roy had said was true. Was she really seeing Ken because it looked cool to hang around with his group of friends? Then she would get mad at herself for paying so much attention to *anything* Roy Harris said. She would try to put it out of her mind and just focus on having a good time with Ken. But little by little, Roy's haunting words kept creeping back.

Kathy had barely paid attention to the movie. It was about some high school guy who was a computer whiz. One day when he was home sick from school with a cold, he started taking over the world with his computer. Kathy thought it was extremely boring, but Ken seemed to really like it.

After the movie one of Ken's friends suggested that they meet up at the Pizza Hut, for a snack.

"Sounds good to me. I'm starved," Ken said. "How about you, Kathy?"

"Uh—I don't think so, Ken," Kathy said. She didn't feel like being with his friends any longer. She just couldn't act herself around them, and it was uncomfortable for her. "I really should get home early tonight. I have a lot of work to do tomorrow at home."

"Oh, sure, I'll take you straight home then," Ken said agreeably.

On the way back to the inn they talked about the movie, but seemed to have completely opposite feelings about it.

" . . . And that part when he uses the computer to control the Russian missiles was great," Ken said, enthusiastically praising every scene.

"Oh, yeah—that was pretty good," Kathy agreed in a much less spirited voice.

"Well, I guess you have to know something about computers to really appreciate it," Ken added. "Deena told me you guys have one at home. Ever fool around with it?"

"Uh—no. Computers kind of give me a rash," Kathy said with a half-hearted smile.

That was another thing about Ken; sometimes he just started rambling on and on about the most boring subjects. Kathy would feel herself spacing out, but she couldn't help it. Like when he started talking about snow, for instance. She hoped he wasn't going to start in on computers now. She might as well have gone out on a date with Deena. Luckily, the inn was in sight.

"Well, here we are," Ken said, shutting off the engine. "Are you going to be busy painting all weekend? I was wondering if you wanted to go hiking on Sunday afternoon."

"Hiking?" Kathy blurted out. This relationship wasn't romance—it was an endurance test. She had barely survived the skiing . . . and then last week Ken had taken her on a marathon bike ride. Finally, Kathy knew what she had to do.

"I have to hang around the inn and help out on Sunday, too, Ken."

"Oh, O.K. Maybe I'll stop by and say hello on my way back."

"O.K., that would be nice." Kathy bit down on her lip. "Gee—on second thought, I don't know if you should." Ken didn't move a muscle, but she felt the space between them crackle with tension. Kathy took a deep breath. She didn't want to hurt Ken's feelings, but she had to do the right thing.

"Listen, you know I really like you, Ken, and we really have a good time together and all. But sometimes I think we're just too different. Into different things, I mean." Kathy glanced over at him. He was staring down at the steering wheel with a thoughtful expression. "You know what I mean?" she asked in a quiet voice.

He looked over at her and nodded, then looked straight ahead again. "I was . . . well, kind of getting that feeling myself the past few days."

There was a long moment of silence, and Kathy thought she should say something. "But even if people are different . . . they can still be good friends. Don't you think?"

"Oh, sure." He gave her a smile. "And we're already good friends, Kathy. Right?"

"Right." Kathy nodded. She reached over and squeezed his hand. "Good night, Ken. Thanks for the movie . . . and everything."

He nodded. "Sure, it was fun. See you in school, O.K.?"

"Sure. See you." Kathy opened the car door and ran out. When she got to the porch, she turned around and waved to Ken. He waved back and drove away.

Chapter 9

"You can put a second coat on that door, and I'll do this piece of trim," Deena said, handing Kathy the correct size paintbrush for her job. "Then we'll be all finished."

It was late Saturday morning. They had gotten an early start on the hallway, and Deena could hardly believe how fast she and Kathy had painted this morning. Kathy, however, did not seem half as thrilled with their progress.

"Great," she replied in a dull voice. She sighed and, without further comment, got to work on the door.

Deena didn't understand what was wrong. She knew Kathy wasn't upset about their fight last night. After all, *she* was the one who had gotten hit with the paint roller. Why should Kathy still be in a mood over that today?

Kathy had really been acting strange. She had been meek as a lamb all morning, doing whatever Deena said without one snide comment or wisecrack. She didn't even complain when Deena asked if she could put a Vivaldi concerto on the tape player. Kathy normally went bananas at the mere mention of classical music. But she had just shrugged, and didn't even seem aware that Deena had advanced from Vivaldi, to Bach, to Mozart.

"How was the movie last night?" Deena asked, in an effort to get Kathy out of her blue mood.

"Oh, it was all right. Actually, I thought it was pretty boring, but Ken seemed to like it."

Kathy sighed and kept painting the door. Resolved to be nicer to her cousin, Deena figured talking about Ken would surely cheer Kathy up.

"Maybe the next time Ken comes over, you can rent a movie you both like," she encouraged.

"Ken won't be coming over for a while," Kathy said in a very matter-of-fact tone.

"Oh? Really?" Deena tried to act calm and casual, but looking down, she noticed that she had just painted over the toe of her right sneaker. "Did you guys have a fight or something?"

"No—nothing like that. But we both thought that it would be better from now on if we were just friends. Ken is a real nice guy," she added, "but we really don't have that much in common. I mean, it wasn't like hanging out with—" Kathy stopped herself. Just short of admitting she really missed Roy, Deena guessed. "Well, with someone who's really on your wavelength."

"I know what you mean," Deena replied quickly. Wasn't that the way she felt about Ken?

Deena focused her attention back to painting. Now she felt worse than ever about being jealous of Kathy and Ken, and worse still about fouling up things between Kathy and Roy.

The Mozart sonata finished, and Deena went inside to change the tape. When she came back, Kathy was staring at her, wide-eyed.

"Do you realize what you just put on the tape player?" Kathy asked her.

Deena nodded. "Sure—Nuclear Waste. The *Totally Wasted Live* album. I thought you liked this?"

"Uh—I do," Kathy nodded, looking confused. "Maybe we should open another window in here. Are you feeling dizzy or anything like that, Deena? I heard that paint fumes can cause brain damage."

Deena wiped her hands on a rag and glared at her. Kathy was starting to sound like her old smart aleck self again. "Nothing for *you* to worry about, however," Deena retorted with a smile. "To be in any danger, first a person needs a brain."

When Kathy and Deena had completely finished, their mothers came upstairs to admire their work. They both agreed that it was a beautiful, professional-looking job and couldn't have been better if they'd hired real house painters.

"What's left on the list, Mom?" Deena asked, eager to get started on a new project. "I bet we're almost done with everything."

"Oh, don't I wish, honey," Lydia said with a worried frown. She glanced down at the work list, then back at the others. "Even if we finish all these repairs, there's still all the cooking and preparing of the guest rooms to be done. I just don't know if we'll make it by Thursday."

Aunt Nancy had been trying to fix a leaky pipe in one of the bathrooms all morning without much success. Her clothes and face were streaked with grease, and she was still carrying around a big wrench, for lack of any convenient place to put it down.

"Listen, Lydia—we need to call in some help here. We'll never get done in time otherwise. Look, I picked up this flier in Henderson's Hardware this morning. What do you think?" She pulled out a folded piece of paper from her back pocket and showed it to everyone.

Kathy immediately recognized the flier as Roy's. It read, "If it ain't broke, don't fix it. But when it is—call MR. FIX-IT. Painting, plumbing, yard work. You name it, we do it. Fast and reliable. Super-low prices." Then at the bottom there was a number to call.

"I like the slogan," Kathy's mother said with a little laugh.

"I like the part about the super-low prices," Deena's mother said. "I guess we should call and speak to this Mr. Fix-it. Whoever he is—"

"He's Roy," Kathy blurted out, before she had a chance to think.

"Roy Harris?" Deena's mother frowned. "Oh—well, that's the end of that. Any other suggestions?"

"You mean you're not going to call, just because it's

Roy?" Deena asked. Finally, here was a chance for Kathy to smooth things over with Roy. She couldn't let her mother ruin everything. Besides, they needed the help. "I don't think that's fair, Mother, and we could really use the help. I'm sure Roy knows what he's doing, just like the flier says," she finished.

"Deena's right, Lydia," Kathy's mother agreed. "We do need the help. We could at least give him a try on something small to start. Like the leaky pipe I've been wrestling with all morning."

Deena's mother looked surprised, especially by her daughter. But she knew she'd been outnumbered.

"All right, have Mr. Fix-it come over right now, if you insist," she said, tossing up her hands. "But I can't imagine that Roy Harris is *fast* and *reliable* at anything but causing trouble. Sorry to say so, Kathy. But that's just the way I feel."

Kathy dug her hands in the pockets of her overalls. Even though she was still mad at Roy, she didn't like hearing him unfairly criticized by Aunt Lydia. She had been amazed and pleased that Deena, of all people, had spoken up for him. Aunt Lydia never gave Roy a fair chance. Now maybe she'd see that he wasn't some irresponsible space cadet, riding around on a motorcycle, trying to act tough.

"Well, I guess we'll see, Aunt Lydia," Kathy said quietly.

Kathy hoped Roy would do a good job and show everybody. But she wondered where she could hide while he was doing it.

Kathy's mother called Roy and told him what type of work they needed done. A half hour later he was standing at the back door with a bag of tools and supplies, looking very serious and very handy—as well as handsome, Kathy thought. She barely mumbled hello to him, then made herself scarce.

Nancy showed him the leaky pipe, and he got to work on it immediately. Less than half an hour later, he announced that it was fixed. Lydia picked out some other jobs on the list—a broken light switch in one of the guest rooms and a cracked pane of glass that needed to be replaced. Then there were various drippy faucets in different parts of the inn that also needed attention. While Roy changed washers, rewired, and adjusted faucets with the air of a guy who really knew his stuff, both mothers whispered to each other down in the kitchen.

"The kid is unbelievable—he's a one-man maintenance crew," Nancy said. "Do you see the way he handles that wrench?"

"And he doesn't waste a minute. I would have never believed it if I hadn't seen it with my own eyes," Lydia agreed. "At this rate Mr. Fix-it is going to finish off this repair list by suppertime. And to think I almost didn't want you to call him."

Deena was glad that she had persuaded them to take a chance on Roy. And she was pleased—not to mention surprised—at how well he was working out. But the whole point of this had been to get Roy and Kathy to-gether *talking* again. And unfortunately, ever since Roy had arrived, Kathy had transformed herself into the Amazing Invisible Cousin.

However, Deena had gotten this far and she wasn't about to give up now. So while Roy was out on the roof, examining a hole that needed to be tarred over, Deena sneaked up to the attic and quietly closed and locked the window that he had used to get up there.

She and Kathy were making up the beds in the guest rooms on the second floor when the banging started a short while later. Softly at first, then louder.

"What in the world is that?" Kathy said, dropping a pillow and listening for the strange sounds coming from the attic.

"What?" Deena pretended she didn't hear anything. "What are you talking about?"

"That noise in the attic. Listen . . . hear it?"

Deena shrugged. "Squirrels?"

Kathy gave her a look. Roy was calling for help now, and the sound was unmistakable. "It's Roy. He's stuck on the roof."

"Sounds like it," Deena said lightly.

"Well . . . " Kathy looked at her. "Do you think we should let him just freeze out there?"

"Of course not." Deena made no motion, however, to go up to the attic and let him back in. "Besides, the roof is pretty slippery. He might fall off running around up there."

"Deena—could you come down here a minute? We need your help," Lydia called from downstairs.

For once, perfect timing! Deena thought. "Coming . . . "

She smiled at Kathy, who had the look of someone left with a particularly irksome task to do. "You'd better go let him in, Kathy, before our mothers find him stuck out there. It wouldn't do much for Mr. Fix-it's 'fast and reliable' reputation."

Kathy headed up to the attic, stopping in her bedroom to quickly comb out her thick brown hair. She looked kind of messy today—but what did it matter? Mr. Fix-it thought she was a status-seeking creep.

Kathy opened the window and let Roy in. He looked relieved to be rescued, even if it was by Kathy.

"Gosh—I can't understand how that happened. The window must have slipped closed when I wasn't looking. Guess I'd better take a look at that, too."

"Guess so," Kathy said nervously. She rubbed her hands together, wondering how the window had managed to slip closed and *lock* itself. She had a sneaking suspicion that Deena knew something about that. She'd ask her about that later.

"That hole isn't so bad. I could patch it up. Good enough to last through one winter, anyway."

"Really? The roofer wanted to charge my mother and aunt a fortune to fix it," Kathy confided to Roy, forgetting for the moment that she was mad at him, and that he probably despised her.

"It just needs a patch and some tar. I brought everything over."

Before Kathy knew it, she was suddenly Mr. Fix-it's new helper, handing him tools back and forth through the attic window, making sure he didn't back up too far and fall off the roof. They didn't exchange much conversation, and what there was of it had to do with the task at hand. But Kathy had to admit to herself that despite the awkward situation, being with Roy made her feel kind of nice inside.

Just as Roy was finishing up, Kathy's mother came up to the attic and told him to come down to the kitchen for a snack. When Roy and Kathy entered the kitchen, everyone was sitting around the big oak table, sampling the cranberry muffins Nancy had just taken out of the oven. The kitchen smelled wonderful and felt warm and cozy. Now that most of the hard work was out of the way, Kathy could feel herself getting excited about the big Thanksgiving Day party.

"Have a seat, Roy," Lydia said cheerfully. "What can I get for you? We have some fresh apple cider. Or maybe you'd like soda? I'll bet you're hungry after all that work. How about a sandwich?"

For a minute Roy looked like he thought someone was playing a joke on him. Deena's mother had never even liked him to come into the house—now she was just about offering to cook him a seven-course meal. Kathy almost burst out laughing.

"Some cider would be fine," Roy said shyly. He took a seat at the end of the table next to Johnny.

Deena's mother brought Roy a glass of cider and sat down. Since the only empty seat left was next to Roy, Kathy drank her cider standing by the kitchen counter.

"Thank you for coming by on such short notice today, Roy," Lydia said. "You really did a great job. I'm going to recommend you to all my friends."

"Yeah—great pinch-hitting, Roy," Johnny said, taking a huge bite out of his muffin.

Roy smiled shyly. "No problem. Thanks for calling me in to help."

"Lydia and I were wondering if you could come over again on Thanksgiving Day for a few hours to help out," Kathy's mother said. Kathy nearly choked on her cranberry muffin. "This place is going to be a zoo with the party going on. And all of our guests will have checked in by then. We could certainly use an extra hand."

Roy glanced over at Kathy. She looked down into her cup and took a sip. "Sure—I can come by. It sounds like it will be fun."

"Great. Now I want to show you something, everybody," Deena's mother said brightly. "Just look at all the check marks on this list! Isn't it gorgeous?"

She held up her famous list and showed them that practically every job was now checked off. Even though she was quite serious, everyone else started laughing.

"I can't believe you, Aunt Lydia," Kathy said.

"When you're done with that infamous list, Lydia, please give it to me," her sister said. "I'm going to have it framed and give it back to you as a Christmas present."

Everyone at the table started laughing again, and Kathy stole a glance at Roy. He was looking at her, too. He smiled—that same old Roy Harris smile—and slowly but surely, she smiled back.

Chapter 10

On Thanksgiving morning everyone at the inn was up bright and early. This is almost as bad as going on a ski trip, Kathy thought as she dragged herself out from under her nice warm covers. Her mother, aunt, and Deena were already downstairs working. Even Johnny was counting out pieces of silverware at the dining room table. Her mother and aunt had hired a cook and two other women to help with the rooms and serving meals. But there was still plenty of work to be done.

The morning flew by in a hectic whirlwind of last-minute preparations. Deena and Kathy were upstairs getting dressed when the last weekend guests arrived to check in. All the others had come on Wednesday. The two girls ran to the window in their room to get a look at the stragglers. It was an older couple, but all Deena and Kathy could make out from the third floor was that they both had silver-gray hair and tweed topcoats.

"They look like somebody's grandparents," Kathy said.

Deena laughed. "They probably are."

"I don't know. I just don't get it. I mean, I can't believe people are actually going to *pay* to stay here," Kathy said, staring at Deena.

"You mean you just figured that out?" Deena shook her head and zipped up her white wool pleated skirt. "Sometimes I really think you're in outer space."

Deena pulled on her sweater, which was peach-colored angora wool with a lace collar at the rounded neckline. She picked out a gold heart-shaped locket on a chain and small gold earrings from the jewelry box on her dresser. Then she brushed out her hair and put on a touch of mascara and some lip gloss.

Kathy was almost ready, too. She was wearing her black leather miniskirt and a hot-pink cotton sweater that looked great with her dark hair and eyes. She had wanted to wear her banana earrings, but Deena talked her out of it, saying that she didn't think the guests were ready for such a treat on their very first day at the inn. Kathy made a face, but did change them for a pair of plain silver hoops.

The two girls went downstairs together. Other guests and friends from town were entering in a steady stream through the front door, and the front parlor and dining room were filled with people as well. Roy was carrying some suitcases upstairs, and Kathy and Deena passed him in the hallway.

"I think these people brought a load of bricks with them," he mumbled under his breath. "How much did they pack? They're only staying for the weekend."

"Gripe, gripe, gripe," Kathy shook her head and turned to Deena. "You just can't get reliable help these days, Deena."

"What do you want for *super-low* prices?" Deena replied.

Laughing, Roy lugged the suitcases upward. Kathy couldn't help noticing that along with a pair of jeans and a clean white shirt, Roy had even put on a tie for the occasion. It was hanging a little loosely around his neck. But she knew that even Aunt Lydia would give him an A for effort.

The party went along very smoothly, thanks to more of Lydia's careful planning and meticulous lists. Deena and Kathy served hot hors d'oeuvres and drinks. Later they helped set up the huge Thanksgiving buffet in the dining room and made sure all their guests had everything they needed. The table was filled with all kinds of delicious holiday food—a huge roasted turkey and a ham, baked sweet potatoes, homemade cranberry sauce, three different vegetables prepared in fancy recipes, and a variety of homemade breads and desserts.

It was well after midnight when the last guest went home, and those staying over at the inn retired to their rooms.

"What a blast, Lydia!" Kathy's mother said, flopping

into a kitchen chair. "I think we were a smashing success. I bet we'll get headlines in the *Cranford Gazette*."

Deena's mother turned from the sink, her hands covered with soap. "Everyone seemed to have had a good time," she said. "I think we'll get some good word-of-mouth advertising from folks in town."

Deena yawned. Her feet were aching from being up on them for so long all day, and she couldn't wait to go to bed. "Can we finish cleaning up tomorrow?" she asked her mother. "I'm pooped."

"You can go ahead up if you want, honey," her mother said. "But most of this disaster area has to be straightened out tonight. We have guests staying with us now, remember?"

"Oh—right." She had forgotten for a second. After changing into her jeans and sneakers, Deena came back downstairs again and helped finish cleaning up the party mess.

Together, she, Kathy, and Roy quickly put the parlor and dining room back in order. Roy took out a few gigantic bags of trash, then grabbed his leather jacket off the hook near the kitchen door.

"Good night, Roy," Deena said, going up the kitchen stairs. "Thanks for helping us today."

"Good night, Deena," Roy said. Kathy thought she seemed in an awful hurry all of a sudden. Now that she and Roy were all alone in the kitchen, she felt a little nervous. It had been loads easier to talk to him with lots of people around all day. But now she was remembering that they had never really made up after their argument. Was he still mad at her? she wondered.

"Well—I guess I'd better be going," Roy said, putting on his jacket. "The party was really fun. And the food was great, too . . . Did you really make that pumpkin pie, Manelli?"

Kathy could hardly believe her ears. Roy was calling her Manelli again. Just like the old days. It must have meant he wasn't mad at her anymore.

She smiled and nodded. "Well, Deena helped me with the crust. But I mashed up the pumpkin and did the other stuff."

"It was great."

"Thanks." Kathy folded her arms and then unfolded them. She didn't know what else to say. "You want a piece to take home? I think there's a load of it left."

Even though Roy had liked it, Kathy's pumpkin pie hadn't been quite as popular as some of the other desserts.

"O.K. I'll take a piece," Roy said.

Kathy went over to the counter and got out the pie, a paper plate, and some aluminum foil. She was slicing off a big wedge when Roy said, "Hey, I almost forgot, but I have this extra ticket for the Pinheads concert on Saturday night. And I was wondering, if you were going to be back from your *other* plans in time, if you still wanted to go?"

Kathy nearly dropped the slice of pie on her foot. "I—umm—my *other* plans got canceled."

"They did?"

"Uh-huh." Kathy nodded without looking up at Roy.

"You want to go to the concert then? With me . . . and everybody, I mean?"

"Yeah—I'd really like that, Roy." Kathy smiled as she started wrapping up the pie. "You know how I feel about the Pinheads."

"And guess who's playing with them," Roy said excitedly. "The Brain Police. Is that beyond belief, or what?"

"You're kidding!" Two of her very favorite groups, playing together on the very same night. This was too great for words. "Hey, Roy . . . how did you happen to get hold of an extra ticket?"

Roy shrugged and took his slice of pumpkin pie. "I just did, that's all . . . Guess you are one lucky Pinheads fan."

"Yeah—Pinheads unite . . . "

" . . . And rock all night," Roy said with a smile. He pulled up his collar, walked to the back door, and opened it. Then he suddenly turned around, walked back to Kathy, and kissed her quickly on the cheek.

"Good night, Roy," Kathy said, feeling a little stunned.

"Good night, Manelli," he called back over his shoulder. Kathy watched from the kitchen window as he kicked down the clutch on his motorcycle and flew off into the night.

***

The next morning life around the inn was quite confusing with eight real-live guests to take care of. Kathy's mother took charge of directing traffic in the kitchen, while Deena's mother made sure everything was going smoothly out in the dining room—smoothly as could be expected on their first morning.

Because they were still shorthanded, Deena and Kathy had to fill in as temporary waitresses. It was Deena's job to serve breakfast, and Kathy's job to clear. Deena was so bubbly and cheerful that Kathy thought she was going to barf. And if Deena wasn't annoying enough, the guests made Kathy crazy.

Everybody was asking for things at once. "Miss, could I have some more coffee, please?" Or "Can these eggs be cooked more?" Or "These eggs are like rubber. Can I have pancakes instead?"

Kathy felt like dumping a bowl of strawberry preserves over somebody's head. Deena, however, was Miss Cool and just smiled and dashed off into the kitchen to get whatever anyone wanted.

"Kathy, stop looking like such a grump. You're going to give the guests indigestion," Deena whispered to her in the kitchen.

"Don't these people have homes of their own?" Kathy whispered back. "Why did they drive all the way to the middle of nowhere to complain about this poor, defenseless dish of scrambled eggs? I think they're perfectly fine scrambled eggs."

Deena just shook her head with that my-cousin-is-completely-hopeless look Kathy knew so well. Then she shoved a basket of toast and muffins into Kathy's hands. "Remember, serve from the left, clear from the right."

After breakfast had ended, Deena and Kathy were clearing off the dining room table when the doorbell rang.

"I'll get it," Kathy said, running into the hallway.

She pulled open the door and was surprised to see Ken standing there. "Hi, Kathy. I notice the inn is open for business. I hope I'm not interrupting anything."

Poor Ken. He must be really taking their breakup a lot harder than she had thought, not being able to leave her alone like this. Kathy had never considered herself a heartbreaker, but obviously poor Ken just couldn't forget her. He had probably dropped by to try and persuade her to go out with him again. Kathy's mind raced, searching for a way to let him down easy.

"No, not at all. Come on in." Kathy let Ken in and then closed the door. "We're just finishing up breakfast. Some of those guests take forever. They eat like it's their last meal," she added in a hushed voice.

Ken laughed. "Maybe they'll eat faster at lunchtime."

"Maybe." Kathy was wearing an apron over her jeans and she wiped her hands on it. What was she going to say when he asked her out again? Too bad he had such a big crush on her. Plenty of other girls would like to go out with him—even if she really didn't, Kathy thought sympathetically.

"Is Deena around?" Ken asked, breaking into her thoughts.

"Deena? Uh, sure. She's in the kitchen."

"I dropped by to see her—to give her these sign-up forms for the ski trip," Ken explained, showing Kathy a big yellow envelope. "Deena's in charge of the finances for the trip on Saturday."

"Oh." Kathy realized she had jumped to all the wrong conclusions about "poor" Ken. "Wait here a minute— I'll go get her for you," Kathy told him.

So, he wasn't heartbroken and pining away for her unique and wonderful company. He wasn't even here to see her—he was here to see Deena. I guess I'm just not as unforgettable as I thought, Kathy said to herself. She opened the kitchen door and looked for her cousin.

"Deena, Ken is here to see you," Kathy casually announced. She picked up a cold piece of toast and took a noisy bite.

"Ken Buckly?" Deena spun around and stared at her. "To see me?"

With her mouth full, Kathy could only nod. "About some forms for the ski club?" she mumbled.

"Oh . . ." Deena raced toward the door, then stopped to pull off her apron and smooth down her sweater. "This sweater has a spot on it. Strawberry preserves," she moaned. "I'm going up to change. Tell him I went to get the list, and I'll be down in a minute, O.K.?"

Without waiting for Kathy's reply, Deena raced up the back staircase. Kathy sat down at the kitchen table, munching on her toast. All of a sudden it was as if a light bulb flashed on over her head. Deena had a crush on Ken! How had she missed it all this time? It all made sense now . . . the way Deena had acted on the ski trip, and how crazy she got when Ken dropped by that first time, and the way she'd been dragging herself around the house these past two weeks . . .

Realizing now how upset it must have made Deena to see her with Ken, Kathy really felt bad. And the truth was that Deena and Ken were a perfect match. Deena had so much more in common with a guy like Ken than Kathy ever would. But she had been so wrapped up in her own problems, she had missed seeing it.

Lost in thoughts about this astounding realization, Kathy got up from the table and finished cleaning up the kitchen by herself. She had just turned on the dishwasher when Deena practically floated back in the room. She was actually glowing.

"Kathy—you didn't have to do all this work by yourself. You could have waited for me," Deena said sweetly as she glanced around the clean kitchen.

"It wasn't so bad," Kathy replied. She'd really felt like doing something nice for Deena after causing her so many problems lately. But she just couldn't admit that out loud.

"Well, I'm going inside to work on the computer for a little while. I have to add these names to the list, and then run off a few copies for the trip tomorrow. Ken is picking me up very early tomorrow morning," Deena added, and Kathy couldn't help noticing the great pleasure her cousin seemed to take in making that announcement.

As Deena floated out of the room, Kathy smiled to herself. It looked as if things were going to work out between Deena and Ken, and Kathy felt truly happy for her cousin.

Later that afternoon Kathy came into the bedroom and was shocked at the strange sight on Deena's side of the room. It was wall to wall clothes—a bona fide mess! Kathy stood in the doorway with her mouth hanging open. The funny thing was that for once, Kathy's side of the room was perfectly neat. Earlier that day she'd been overtaken by the rare impulse to clean up her territory. Partly because she thought it was one way she could be nicer to Deena—although she would never have admitted that aloud.

Just then Deena scurried in from the bathroom. Her hair was pinned back and she had green stuff smeared all over her face. Glancing at Kathy, she seemed suddenly self-conscious. "It's an aloe-mint facial," she explained before Kathy asked. "I—uh—thought I saw a pimple."

"A pimple? You never get pimples," Kathy said in a reassuring tone. Poor Deena. She was usually so together, so in control. Kathy thought her cousin looked kind of cute with that stuff on her face, all worked up over some nonexistent blemish. For once she seemed vulnerable and not so perfect. Kathy felt almost protective of her.

"No, there really was. Right on my chin." Deena walked over to the mirror and checked her chin again.

"I'm sure it's microscopic. You can borrow my coverstick. No one will notice," Kathy said.

"Hmmm. I hope," Deena murmured. Looking at the mirror, she picked up a yellow sweater and held it up in front of her, then picked up a blue one and, with a frown, tossed both on the bed.

"I like the yellow one," Kathy offered, even though she hadn't been asked.

"You do?" Deena was rummaging through the clothes on her bed and gave Kathy a surprised look. The girls rarely gave each other fashion advice, mostly because they never had anything nice to say.

Kathy nodded. "It's a great color for you."

"Thanks." Deena sat down on her bed, holding the yellow sweater in her lap. She blinked, noticing for the first time that Kathy's side of the room had been cleaned up. "What happened over there? I can actually see your bed."

Kathy shrugged. "I don't know. I just got in a clean-up mood or something. Maybe it's a full moon."

"Maybe," Deena said. She picked up one of the many sweaters on her bed and began folding it up neatly to be put away. "For once my side looks like it's been hit by a tornado," she said with a laugh. "Too bad we can't coordinate this better."

"Here, I'll help you fold those." Kathy came over and picked up a sweater, trying her best to fold it as neatly as Deena did. It was certainly a challenge.

Deena was so surprised she didn't know what to say. "Hey—thanks." She gave Kathy a wide smile.

Kathy smiled back. "Don't look now, but your face is cracking," she said.

Deena looked in the mirror and saw that her facial was starting to look like a jigsaw puzzle. "Wow! I look like I visited a space alien beauty salon!"

"You said it, I didn't," Kathy said with a laugh. Then the two girls started laughing together, overtaken by a new fit of giggles every time they looked at Deena's green face.

"Hey—is this a private party, or can anyone join in?"

Kathy and Deena looked up to see both of their mothers standing in the doorway. "Oh, hi, Mom," Kathy said between laughs. "Come on in."

"We just wanted to thank both of you for all the hard work you've done these past few weeks," Lydia said to her daughter and niece. "Our Grand Opening has been such a success . . . "

"And we couldn't have done it without you two, honestly," Nancy finished, giving both girls a hug.

"Well . . . thanks," Kathy said. "It wasn't so bad." Then she suddenly thought of the day she'd smacked into Deena with the paint roller. "Most of the time."

"There were some . . . sticky moments," Deena agreed. "But it was kind of fun."

"Well, we're very proud of you," Lydia added. "And it's nice to see you two getting along so well, for once. What have you been laughing about in here?"

"The space alien beauty salon," Deena said to her mother.

Her mother and aunt exchanged a bewildered glance. But when Deena looked over at Kathy, they started to crack up all over again.

Kathy knew that she and Deena were as different as night and day—and that they would probably always drive each other crazy. But sometimes it was fun to just go crazy together—for a change.